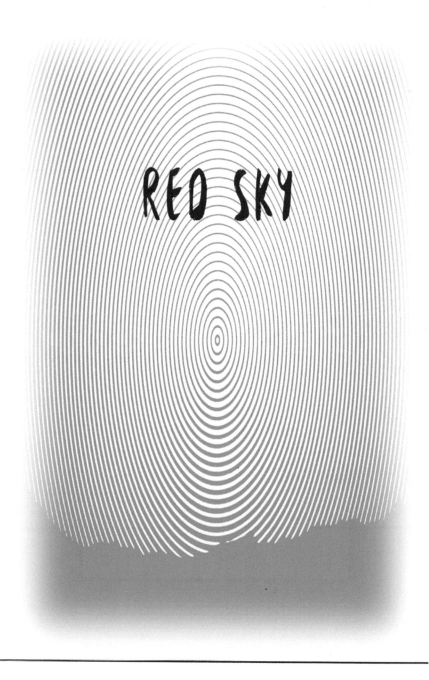

RED SKY

For 'kota.

Preface

To the person holding this book I first and foremost want to say thank you. Thank you so much for taking your time to read the pages that follow. What you are holding is my first but certainly not final attempt at writing. My greatest wish is that what I've written is enjoyed by those that read it though I know I cannot please everyone. So, I welcome comments both of a positive nature and of a more critical nature; I figure this is one of the best ways for my writing to improve. I have even provided my personal email address on the preceding page for readers to share with me what they liked, loved, and hated.

This book is the beginning of my own dream to be a writer, a dream I've had since grade school. In fact, while growing up in northern Wisconsin I would often write short horror stories to scare classmates that shared my hour-long school bus ride.

After high school I found myself lost and confused when it came to the path of my own life so I settled into a career as an auto mechanic. While a sometimes lucrative and always in demand trade it did nothing to quell my need to express myself creatively. In the spring of 2012 I, along with my girlfriend and our two cats, embarked on a seven month journey across the United States. Living in our van we travelled to nearly all four corners of the country and it was on this cathartic journey that the story you are about to read was born.

I know that the story that follows is not perfect even though I have spent the past few years going through countless personal edits while also enlisting friends and family to spot weak areas and mistakes; the entire time learning as I went. All-in-all I hope to scare you a little and in the very least entertain you. This book is entirely an independent work made possible by the support from my friends, family, and readers like you. All I could ask in return is that you tell your friends, rate it, email your thoughts, give it away, lend it, share it, and hopefully enjoy it.

Thanks again,

Kirk Klinger

One

Kyle closed his cell phone slowly, hoping that the tinny voice-mail recording would be interrupted by his mother or father's voice. It wasn't and never would be and this would be the final time he tried calling them. A month had passed since he last spoke to either of them, which was beyond strange if you knew the relationship Kyle and Sandi shared. Kyle had always been incredibly close with both his parents, especially his mother, who worried nearly to the point of needing medication and spoke with her only son almost daily to keep any unknowing from her mind. It was that unknowing, blank spaces in what she knew for sure, that could be filled in with any number of worst-case scenarios and once a thought was started it only picked up speed like a snowball on a steep hill. Jack, his father, was nearly the opposite and only spoke to Kyle during football season to complain about the Packers or just occasionally to say a fatherly 'how's it going?'

It was May 26th that Kyle was first unable to reach anyone at his parents' house, the same house in rural Weirgor, WI he had lived for the first eighteen years of his life, and on the evening of May 27th the police report was filed. Even on the rare occasion that his parents left their home, for the monthly shopping run to Eau Claire or the obligatory appearance at one of Sandi's friends' parties, they were never too late in returning. Jack almost

8

exhibited some anti-social sentiments and was adamant about not getting home any later than eight P.M., he only seemed truly happy at his home, on his land, on his dead-end road in the middle-of-nowhere-Wisconsin.

The night of May 26th Kyle called to complain to his mother about his latest attempt at procuring a girlfriend, he didn't really have any close friends and the friends he did have he always thought of as the "fair-weather" kind. The girl that was to be the topic of conversation was Julie, an uptown Minneapolis hipster. Kyle took the breakup fairly hard like he did with pretty much every breakup he had. In his pursuit of a girl that would be interested in him for more than a couple weeks, he latched onto just about every decent looking female that even said hello to him. As he had always done, he called his mother to vent but she didn't answer.

His frustration at not receiving an answer to his calls quickly turned to fear (he definitely inherited some of his mother's neurosis) and the topic of Julie was long forgotten. Being the small town it was, Weirgor's tiny police force knew and (for the most part) was friendly with Kyle's parents so when Kyle reported his parents missing they seemed to take his concern seriously. By the time the calendar said 'June 25th', Kyle was no closer to knowing his parents' whereabouts than he was the night he made his tearful missing persons report.

Kyle slipped his cheap little cell phone back into the left front pocket of his jeans. He felt like crying again, he'd definitely cry if he knew they were dead but this situation was strange and he still wasn't sure if crying was in order. The feeling that something was incredibly wrong had grown with every scenario he was able to dream up and pretty much all the scenarios seemed stupid and silly when scrutinized. These were the two people that had raised him, two people he had known since the very day of his birth. His mind had searched and searched for any tiny clue as to where they may have gone, any small thing his mother may have mentioned even any change in tone or mood his mother may have shown but really there were no clues. Even the detectives assigned to his parents' case had absolutely nothing; all their belongings had been found at home untouched, his mother's purse, both their vehicles tucked neatly away in the garage, suitcases remained unpacked in their closet-nothing seemed out of place. He even caught himself trying hard to think of someone who may want to harm his parents but he came up with no one.

He plopped himself down into the only piece of furniture he had in his tiny apartment, an older, brown LaZ Boy recliner he got second hand from his parents. If someone had seen him they would have told him he looked like someone who had just given up.

His apartment was depressingly small and contained only an old television, a couple gaming consoles, his old bed from home, his recliner, and a few other things he had moved from the bedroom he had back home. At 28 and having been living on his own for nearly ten years, Kyle had little to show for the life he had tried to make mostly because he lacked any sort of direction or drive. His life over the years after he moved from home were mostly filled with moving from apartment to apartment and job to job with periods of binge drinking mixed in. Despite being reasonably intelligent and pretty good with his hands, the only jobs available when he was growing up were on local dairy farms, Kyle just didn't know what he wanted to do with his life and while he was trying to figure that out, ten years passed him up. Some of the jobs he landed were decent ones, ones where he made decent money and could have moved up in quite easily if only they had been able to hold his interest for more than a year or two. He seemed to get bored easily with everything around him, his job, his car, the town and apartment he lived in and usually after a year or so that itch to change the things around him started getting bad. He even got bored with his own reflection and often changed his hairstyle, clothes, and facial hair in an effort to keep that itch for change somewhat scratched.

Currently, he was attempting to let his dark brown hair grow out a little though he would probably soon give up, his hair had always been thin and ended up just looking stringy and flat when it had any length. He also had recently tried growing a mustache but the sparse and uneven hair growing in on his upper lip looked stupid to him and he quickly shaved, opting to instead try growing a small beard. Attempts were made to keep in shape by paying for gym memberships off and on; he figured that if he was paying money for a membership that he would actually use it. Kyle went through times when he would work out steadily but those periods usually petered out (usually sometime after a period of binge drinking) and by the time his parents went missing he hadn't been to a gym or paid for a membership in quite a while.

Kyle sat staring into nothingness, his face drawn and tired looking, usually people would have told him he looked five years younger than twenty-eight but today it would probably have been five years older. The evening sun pouring through the slits of his cheap blinds was starting to fade into a deep orange. With a sigh of sadness and exhaustion he rose slowly from his chair, he looked like someone who had been in decent shape but had let themselves go, a small beer belly bowing the front of his t-shirt and a layer of fat padding over the muscles he had worked so hard to put on.

He made his way into his tiny kitchen where he grabbed a beer from his fridge and took note that there were only three left. The cold beer was cheap and didn't really taste great but lately, he wasn't really drinking beer for its taste and as it slid down his throat he felt some hint of comfort. With the cold beer sweating in his right hand he looked into his apartment, the emptiness and white walls tinted orange from the setting sun, and he wondered

12

what came next. How long before his parents were considered dead? Did they even have a will? He decided that the second thought really didn't matter much since his parents were pretty much all the family he really knew, he did have some aunts, uncles, and cousins but they were all distant and scattered across the U.S. If they had written a will he was sure they would leave what little they had to him.

His parents had never really had much, once again work was hard to come by in middle-of-nowhere-Wisconsin and they had the best jobs they could probably get, but they never really seemed to need much. Both worked hard as Kyle grew up and they never failed to put food in his belly or clothes on his back. What they did have was a small home on about forty acres of land, both of which had been handed down from his father's parents who Kyle had never even been able to meet.

As the orange sun sunk below the horizon, the mostly empty apartment was consumed in shadow, Kyle became a vague silhouette of a man holding a dripping can of beer. He looked from his dark television to the dark form of his chair and to the black and unmistakable shape of his acoustic guitar propped up in one of the four empty corners of his apartment. Nothing held any interest for him now, he didn't want to watch television, he didn't want to play guitar, which was actually a little strange because it was one of the things he really liked doing when feeling depressed, but this was different. Since his parents failed to return his calls he was seldom hungry and only went into work a couple times a week (he probably wouldn't be employed much longer) the only thing he still had a taste for was the momentary warm comfort of alcohol, and this fact kind of scared him. His imagination sparked with a glimpse of himself in the near future; unemployed, living in his parents' empty, sad house, fast on his way to an early death by alcoholism. He thought that he'd probably feel different, better somehow, if he knew they were dead and especially if he could have, at least, said goodbye. The thought that someone could possibly have done something to them sparked one of the only emotions he seemed capable of feeling lately and that was pure fury, he didn't think anyone would have but it seemed like the only explanation that seemed even remotely possible.

Tired, exhausted really, Kyle plopped back down in his chair. He set his now empty beer can on the floor next to him, reclined, and let a fitful sleep overtake him. He dreamt he was a child again back at home with his parents.

***

Once five weeks had passed since Kyle last spoke with his parents, the little hope he may have been clinging to, at this point, had blown away like the few remaining summer leaves in a fall breeze. After having conversations with a few relatives who had sent their utmost, heartfelt condolences but would be unable to attend any kind of funeral, Kyle had decided to have one anyway. Not long after the cheap, impromptu funeral his (now ex) boss, who understood that Kyle was going through a tough thing but still needed him to show up to work on occasion, lost patience. The detectives working on his parents' case, who still had absolutely nothing to go on, seemed to be giving up so Kyle finally decided to return to his parents' home. It seemed like the next step to him, plus he was jobless and would soon be homeless so this would give him a place to go. A voice within him wanted to know why he hadn't gone home the day after they had gone missing, why he hadn't spent weeks doing his own searching, but in lieu of any sufficient excuse all he could offer the voice was his guilt, frustration, and shame. He had just kind of operated on the thought that the next day they would return and all would be fine again, like dealing with the diagnosis of an illness by ignoring it. If he just didn't acknowledge their strange disappearance he wouldn't actually have to admit it was real. He knew these thoughts were dumb and possibly even lazy, in fact he felt dumb for letting so much time pass but pass it did and they were still gone.

During the three-hour drive from his apartment in Minneapolis to his parents' house in Weirgor he tried to shake the depression he had been feeling after his parents' disappearance, he even brought a few things along with him in case he decided to stay a while. Kyle usually loved driving, loved the air in his face, the music blaring from his radio, the power of the car beneath his ass, and today was a perfect day for a drive; green, bright, warm. Despite the beautiful summer weather he just couldn't escape the black cloud that had formed and made the space above his head home, he drove the last two hours with the radio turned down so it was nearly inaudible and the windows rolled up tight. The distance became a necessary chore to accomplish before whatever met him in Weirgor.

It was late afternoon, the summer sun still high and bright in the cloudless sky, as Kyle drove through his tiny hometown. There was a time that didn't seem that long ago when he'd see people he knew but pretty much every face he passed now was that of a stranger; he knew they looked at him in the same way he used to look at "out-of-towners". The road that bisected the town took him slowly past his old grade school, a building now divided into cheap apartments, the farm-field sized playground transformed into only an overgrown patch of open grass and weeds. Everything in the town seemed old, tired, and worn out as he passed; he didn't think this place seemed this way when he was young. There was little interest in this town now, it was populated mostly by the families that had always been here and the railroad money that originally built the town had long ago dried up. People passing through on the small county highway need only blink to miss it all. On the eastern outskirts of the town, he turned onto the dead-end dirt road that would take him to the home he had known during all of his youth. It was a dusty two-mile drive through the dense Wisconsin forest passing only two other houses, both inhabited by older retired couples that his parents had known well before the road just ended right at his parents' front yard. Kyle had always felt pretty lucky to have grown up where he was free to play outside with absolutely no fear of traffic or strangers in windowless vans offering candy, though he probably didn't appreciate his backwoods upbringing as much as he should have until he moved to Minneapolis.

A quarter mile before reaching the house, the dense green woods that closely flanked both sides of the road fell away as two rectangular fields took their place. The fields to either side of him hadn't been used for many years tall grasses and weeds now claimed them. As Kyle's car emerged from the darkness of the overhanging pines and birches, his tires rumbling loudly on the course gravel, into the openness of the large fields he could see his parents' white home sitting as it always had in the middle of a group of pines. As the white home grew in front of him he couldn't help but notice how strikingly beautiful the world around him was, he hadn't been out of the city in quite a while and everything seemed so bright and filled with color. Karma Police was softly playing from the car's tiny speakers. The bright summer sky was a flawless blue that changed from light blue to a deeper sapphire toward the horizon. The sun was still hours from saying goodnight, still high and yellow and the dense vegetation that framed the fields and the house as far as he could see was a deep and lush green. A growing cloud of dust in his wake Kyle slowed his car, as he slowly approached the driveway a great sadness gripped his heart like someone crushing an overripe tomato. Every time, up until now that is, he had pulled into this driveway he knew his visit would be joyous. Visits for holidays or just to enjoy a summer weekend with homemade meals and cold beers.

At one time, long before Kyle had even drawn his first breath, the house was the center of a small farm. All that was left of the farm now was a dilapidated barn and ancient fence posts still entwined with rusty barbed wire. The house was old and definitely not as large as most of the old farmhouses of the area but his parents were proud of it and had kept it up well.

Now, standing in the yard at the front of the house, the only sign that things weren't as they should be was the yard's grass. His father had always kept the yard as green and kempt as a golf course fairway but it was now shaggy and long overdue for a mowing.

Suddenly Kyle wondered what he was even doing there standing in front of his childhood home. A tear slid down his sun-drenched face and evaporated before it made it to the corner of his mouth leaving a salty little trail in its path. He didn't want to even set foot in this house, all his parents' things would be in there. It would smell like them. A tremble worked its way up from his stomach and he was unable to hold back his tears. Kyle was not a man that cried often, he would have been hard-pressed to remember the last time, but on this summer day he did, for a long time.

By the time Kyle felt that he had cried his cry, and gotten out some of what he had been holding on to, he decided he should go inside. This was probably going to be his new home and he wasn't going to get over anything by standing in the yard crying while the exposed parts of his skin blistered with sunburn.

Assuming the front door was locked he decided to grab the spare key his parents always had stashed in the old doghouse in the yard. The large doghouse had housed a number of pets over the years and, even after his parents stopped having dogs, had always been the hiding place for the house key. He reached his hand beneath the doghouse's shingled roof for the small plastic container with the key he had used many times but his hand felt nothing. The small space where the container should be was empty, it was gone. Not putting too much thought into the missing key he decided to simply try the front door, the house was unlocked. Whatever officer or detective was supposed to lock up after doing his investigating had obviously failed to do so. As Kyle opened the front door he expected to see the home that he had always walked into on his visits. What he saw was an unrecognizable mess. He stood in the open doorway as anger welled up inside him. Nothing looked to be missing. His mother's cooking appliances were all there. Their china cabinet in the living room, the little he could see of it, looked relatively untouched. In his angered mind he imagined all the things he would say to investigators that had so needlessly trashed his parents' house. *And for what? What did they really expect to find?* Then the thought that if they had found something that had led to his parents' recovery, cooled him off a little. The sight of the home he loved in shambles was still disappointing.

Sadly making his way deeper into the home, he picked up as he went. Setting knick-knacks back on their shelves and closing drawers and cabinets. Slowly, the loving home of his parents began to look as it once had and how Kyle thought it should. Opening a familiar door, he was happy to see that whatever heavy-handed detective had pawed through the house had left his old room pretty much intact. Well, it had more or less become a storage room for all the things his parents had collected and accumulated but didn't necessarily need right away, the type of room Kyle thought most old houses had. Looking at the collection of papers, a rug shampooer, old magazines and boxes of stuff only his father probably knew the contents of, he saw the few remaining artifacts of his life here. Framing the walls around the far window that looked out onto the back yard was a collection of drawings he had done sometime in high school. Still thumb-tacked to the wall on his left was his coveted black and white Radiohead poster showing only the angry bear with the word "RADIOHEAD" beneath it, and on the wall to his right was a small poster of the X-Men still leftover from the years he spent collecting comic books. Knowing his old room would no longer be of use to him, not without a good day of relocating all the stuff, he made his way into his parents' larger room.

Surprisingly the bed was still made and a pair of his father's work pants were still laid out on the end of the floral print comforter. After picking up a few things around the room and shuffling a pile of papers into the closet, the room looked as if his parents were to arrive home at any moment. That thought took the strength from Kyle's legs; luckily he was close enough for the bed to catch him as he fell. How badly he wanted to think that they were just out shopping and any moment he would hear the light thunder sound of their car coming down the dirt road. He knew they weren't coming home, as badly as he would deny it and hope he was wrong, he felt they were truly gone.

Emotionally exhausted, Kyle fell into a light sleep on his parents' old bed. While he slept, the sun slid its way down the sky and he dreamt of his parents laughing. They were laughing at him, laughing at their son as if they had played a good joke on him, laughed at his tears over them. Their faces floated before him and they just wouldn't stop laughing.

When he awoke the sun was low in the sky and its light was painting the bedroom a dull red, he had left part of the comforter soaked with sweat, and the sound of his parents' cruel laugh still echoed in his ears.

Kyle wiped sweat from his brow as he rose from the bed, he felt sick and somehow more tired than before he fell asleep. The fog of sleep and the strangeness of his dream still plaguing him, he stared out the window of the bedroom. The setting sun painted his tired, sad face a fiery orange. Sliding open the window he knew soon he would hear the summer song of the crickets and frogs, a song he had once loved but now he almost dreaded. He wondered to himself when he would feel different when he would get over this and he decided he never would even though he knew he would have to. This is what so many of those sappy movies were about, the ones that made girls cry and men roll their eyes as they looked for a distraction. Only this wasn't a movie or even some sappy novel like the ones his mother read, this was his life. He didn't feel like the characters in those stories, the ones that changed the direction of their sad lives in the wake of tragedy or personal loss. He didn't feel any cathartic journey unraveling or even the beginnings of a great epiphany, just sadness hardening into apathy.

In an effort to shake the mood he was in, he told himself he was becoming way too "emo", so he decided to lose himself in something on television. 'A good movie' he thought to himself as he plopped himself into the plush lounger that would usually be occupied by his father and picked up the remote control on the end table. None of those sappy, boo-hoo movies he was thinking about a minute ago but probably something funny or maybe one of the action movies that Kyle thought of as almost a form of violence-porn.

Just before Kyle pushed the orange button that would flood the small living room with the glow of television the sun dipped below the forested horizon. The sun's red paint darkened considerably and the shadows in the house grew inky black. 'I need a beer' he thought to himself, a thought he was surprised he hadn't thought before he had even sat down.

The kitchen was shrouded in shadow, only a few maroon highlights remained from the sunset outside. Kyle found one of his father's beers, as he knew he would, in the well-stocked refrigerator. In the rapidly darkening kitchen, he twisted the cap on the brown bottle and took the first pull from it, letting out the sigh one almost always does after taking the first large swallow of a cold beer. Beer in hand he turned to return to his attempt at escapism through the use of Hollywood special effects, but something he saw in his peripheral out of the window above the kitchen sink stopped him. With a look of curiosity twisting his face, he pressed up close to the window above the sink. The small window looked out over the field to the right of the dirt road. At first, he was sure he was seeing things, a trick of the evening light or possibly a white-tail feeding on the far edge of the field but as he stared longer into the fading light he became surer of what he saw. On the far end of the field, just before it became thick forest again, was the tiny, dark silhouette of a person. Chill fingers walked over his spine and his goose-bumped skin glazed over with a slimy sweat, his beer fell into the sink and shattered. Foamy beer and shards of brown glass rained over each side of the sink but Kyle never broke his gaze from that silhouette. The person was staring at him, at the house, he was sure of it. It was only a vague silhouette in the almost complete dark of night but he was sure they were looking toward him. His mind raced with possible explanations; a local kid, one of the neighbors, a trick of his tired eyes, but none of them felt right. The dark shape was motionless as Kyle stared and the-middle-of-nowhere-Wisconsin began to plunge into the darkness that was night. Just before absolute darkness washed the silhouette away, Kyle thought he saw the person run freakishly quick toward the forest to the right of the field where they disappeared into the dense underbrush. He was never really sure how long he continued to stare out that window, scrutinizing every single shadow, but it had to have been quite a long time. He knew it would take quite a while for his nerves to settle.

At around the point when one could stop calling it "night" and would have to start calling it "early-morning" Kyle finally found sleep. After watching two movies, interrupted by checking, futilely, out every dark window for anything. He desperately tried to rinse the image of that running silhouette in the field from his memory. He changed the sheets on his parents' bed and made sure every door was locked tight before he finally lied down and stared at the ceiling. Bathed in the weak glow of the old night-light he had found and plugged into the wall of his new bedroom, it may have even been his when he was a kid, the thoughts of whether or not he'd ever see his parents again were frequently interrupted with the image of the silhouette-man running on an endless loop. Eventually, his tiredness and exhaustion were finally able to overtake his thoughts and sleep took him.

Just a little before sunrise, as Kyle was entering the deepest part of his sleep, the lock on the front door clicked, the handle turned slowly, quietly, and the front door opened. If he had been awake, Kyle would have surely thought his parents had returned, but he wasn't awake and he never saw the thin, shadowy form move through the house like a ghost. He never felt the bed settle just a little more as that figure climbed in with him. He never woke up as a grotesquely thin arm curled around his chest.

Two

If you had asked Kyle what his girlfriend "type" was he probably would have thought hard for a minute or two then just shrugged. Since entering the awkward age where boys stop finding girls annoying and begin finding them to be something to be sought after, his type pretty much included any girl that paid him any attention. Not that he was void of standards but he enjoyed any female contact he could get. From time to time he would find a girl that wasn't turned off by his lack of outward confidence, paralyzing shyness, and quiet demeanor, but over time he always proved unable to sustain any lasting relationship. At twenty-eight, Kyle had decided that a girlfriend was something he needed. Not that he was in any rush to get married and have children, he just thought that the single life was starting to wear a little thin.

Just over a month before he would report his parents missing, Kyle locked eyes with the girl that he would eventually call his mother to discuss.

"Hi. I'm Julie."

Kyle responded, "Hey. I'm Kyle." his voice wavering nervously.

Standing in the dark backroom of his friend Trent's favorite downtown Minneapolis watering hole, Dirty Fishwater's, Kyle was doing one of the things he always dreaded; meeting new people.

He pretty much always met Trent out for beers at Dirty's when he was called upon. He really thought Trent to be one of the coolest people he knew in Minneapolis, having at one time been in a small band. Plus the girls liked him. Trent was tall and thin with long, unkempt dark hair that fell over his blue eyes, both arms were draped in tattooed sleeves that ended just before his wrists. This was so that he could get away with having a "real" job, all he needed was a long-sleeved shirt. Tonight, Trent had called Kyle to hang out at Dirty's with him during a small get-together of some of his coworkers, apparently most of the people he worked with were incredibly dull and most were almost twice his age, so he had wanted to have someone there that would talk about more than just their stupid kids or how sick they were of their significant other. Kyle just figured Trent hadn't been able to get any of his other friends to come out on account that it was a Tuesday, but he was okay with that and jumped at the chance to down a few beers on a night when the bar would be mostly empty. The only thing Kyle somewhat dreaded was meeting Trent's coworkers, at least before he could swallow enough liquid courage.

Three beers already down and most of the coworkers safely introduced, Kyle felt confident any awkwardness was thankfully avoided. That was until he met one of the coworker's roommates named Julie.

By the time Kyle said his 'hey,' he had forgotten her name. His nervous mind had a bad habit of not being able to retain any new information while in the midst of an attractive female, and Julie had struck Kyle as not just attractive but downright beautiful. A girl that he definitely would have said was out of his league, the type of girl that normally he would go great lengths at avoiding a conversation with. With a red mixed drink in her right hand, she seemed to almost glow in the dim, dirty light of the bar. She was slightly taller than Kyle's 5'8", a trait that Kyle usually was too insecure for. Her thick, natural blonde hair was pulled back in a loose ponytail. She wore the uniform of the hipster; a tight plaid shirt, dark jeans and thick, black rimmed glasses, but Kyle thought the look worked on her. He probably would have thought she looked good dressed in a construction worker's clothes really.

After the introductions were out of the way, Kyle, Trent, the coworker Tanya-or-something and her roommate found a small, empty, round table. Kyle's eyes stayed fixed on *what did she say her name was?!* as he found the stool behind him with his empty hand and guided it to its spot under his ass. There was some conversation going on between Tanya-or-something and

28

the beautiful blonde sitting across from him, it was in this conversation that, thankfully, her name was brought up again. Julie or Jules is what she had said when they were introduced. Kyle figured he'd stick with Julie for now if he even got up enough courage to say anything, and he stuck her name into a spot in his brain where he didn't think he'd lose it.

The conversation switched inevitably to Trent and Tanya's workplace. This conversation meant nothing to Kyle and he sat pretending to listen as he quickly emptied his beer and started to feel the alcohol building up in him. He began to find himself noticing tiny things about Julie as she also sat pretending to listen to Trent and Tanya's conversation; her delicate fingers holding a now nearly empty mixed drink, the bright greenish blue of her eyes, the delicate way she politely smiled to hide her disinterest. It was in this near-trance that the voice in Kyle's head spoke up and brought him back like someone being woken from a great dream.

What do you expect to happen? If anything, she and the roommate will probably take Trent home with them.

The thoughts had a sobering effect and immediately Kyle decided he wanted (needed) another beer.

"I'm going to go grab another beer." Kyle said as he slid clumsily from his stool, Trent and Tanya only paused and glanced at him in recognition.

"I'll go with you." Julie announced as she rattled the melting ice in her glass.

Kyle's heart jumped and started racing, he could feel the first tingles of a slimy sweat starting on his brow and his neck. That voice in his head chanting, *'don't say anything awkward!'*

As Kyle and Julie made their short journey to the front of the bar he asked, "What are you drinking? I'll get ya one." A genuine smile curved his lips as he congratulated himself on the smooth execution of his offer. He thought a small thanks to the alcohol in his system for slowing his tongue, a muscle that normally betrayed him around girls.

Julie tittered and answered, "It's a vodka-cranberry. That's very nice of you, thank you." She shot Kyle a smile of thanks and only accepted because of the huge smile that formed on his face after he offered.

Though it was far from busy, within the time it took Kyle to order their two drinks from a seemingly unmotivated bartender, they had completed most of the small talk that comes with meeting someone new. Kyle had learned that Julie was from Eden Prairie, Minnesota, she worked in the payroll department of a large Minneapolis automotive dealership, she was twenty-five years old and she was single. Kyle divulged much of the same information; his life growing up in tiny Weirgor, his current employment at a computer repair company in west Minneapolis and that he too was single. He was surprised at how succinct he could really be in telling his life's story.

Returning to their table they were now caught up in their own conversation and, after a quick pit-stop at the small, old jukebox, stumbled onto the fact that their taste in music was incredibly similar. As Trent and Tanya leaned drunkenly closer to each other their conversation about coworkers and bosses rambled on, Kyle and Julic (well now she told him to call her Jules if he wanted) continued to find common interests in movies and books and other things.

The night was getting close to its end, glasses with the watery remainders of mixed drinks, and empty beer bottles now littered their small table. Their voices louder now despite the bar being nearly empty. The jukebox had played its last song over an hour ago but no one noticed. Trent and Tanya, their conversation having shifted to reality television shows they enjoyed, were rubbing their legs together beneath the table in anticipation of what they were about to go home together and do. Work the next morning would come much too soon and with a cloud of embarrassment and a little shame.

During a rare lull in Kyle's conversation with Jules, his not-quite-drunk-but-close mind raced with the excitement of a little kid about to open his Christmas morning present from Santa. He marveled at how well he was doing, how much he and this beautiful girl seemed to be "hitting it off" as they say. He knew that the alcohol coursing through his system took some of the credit and the alcohol in her system took the rest but he really didn't care, this beat a night of internet porn anytime.

Finally at around 1:00 AM Trent and Tanya decided they could wait no longer. They said their goodnights and, arms slung around each other's waists, stumbled as one out of the bar to hail a cab to Trent's apartment.

Kyle and Jules looked around and noticed that they were the only two left in the bar. Jules turned and said, "Yea I suppose I should go too, I do have to work in the morning." She placed her hand on top of Kyle's as if to say 'sorry'.

Kyle stared, his tongue paralyzed for a moment as his mind screamed '*aaaaaahhhhhhh she's touching my hand!!!!!*' After a little too long of a pause Kyle answered, "That's okay, I have to work too. I suppose I should take a cab home." His whole body felt electrified with excitement as her soft hand seemed to grab his a little tighter.

"I'll make it up to ya this weekend if you're not busy, we can get dinner together or something," Jules said in her sweetest voice as she stared at Kyle through those thick-rimmed glasses, still not lifting her hand from his.

"Uh, yea. Anything. I'm not busy at all." Kyle said a little awkwardly, his voice beginning to waver again with nervousness and excitement.

After an exchange of phone numbers scrawled on bar napkins, Jules leaned down and sweetly kissed Kyle on the cheek. She thanked him for a fun evening and that she looked forward to Saturday and whatever it is they would decide to do. Kyle's face turned red and hot as they walked out of the bar into the cool early-spring air but Jules didn't notice in the neon glow of the beer signs that took up space in the front windows of the bar.

They probably would have shared a cab but they both lived in opposite directions so they said a final goodnight to each other and disappeared into separate cars. Both of them smiled, as they bounced in the back of their cabs, all the way to their empty apartments.

***

Kyle awoke the following morning, his head was screaming and his mouth tasted like chalk. Rising from his bed his head swam sickly and his stomach lurched a little. He had noticed that as he got older it took less and less booze to make him feel like shit the next morning. Flipping on the light in his little bathroom he leaned in toward the mirror above the sink. He decided he looked as tired as he felt, the small lines that had begun forming on his face seemed deeper today, making him look his age if not a little older. He washed his face with ice cold water, tried brushing the foul taste from his mouth and ran a comb through the short length of his straight hair. Feeling slightly more awake as he left the bathroom he reached for his wallet on the nightstand. Beneath his wallet was a clumsily folded bar napkin, he stared at it as the memory of what had happened only a few hours ago flooded back to him in a blinding rush. The memory of the night woke him up like no drug could as he made his way into his kitchen to make breakfast and then head to work (he realized a little later he had to call another cab). During the short cab ride to work his sober mind wasted no time in dissolving any excitement or happiness leftover from his night with Jules. He knew that when he called her this week she'd be sobered up and realize she gave some loser her phone number. He knew she'd make up some excuse as to why she wouldn't make it out this weekend and she'd have an excuse every time he called until he finally gave up calling. What had been nearly giddiness only hours before was now turning to depression as the emptiness of his real life seemed even emptier after his brush with romanticism.

***

It was Thursday, after two dismal days in Kyle's life, that Jules proved his cynical thoughts wrong. He had been prepared to call her that night but she beat him to it. She called shortly after he had arrived home from work and they made a date (her words) to go out Saturday for dinner and then to a small bar that was featuring a local band. Jules had even sounded excited when he spoke to her.

What came after that fantastic first date was a courtship that lasted just over a month. The relationship burned with all the intensity of a cheap firework, bright and hot for merely moments before fizzling out disappointingly. At first, Jules had loved how different Kyle was from all the big city, self-centered, douche-bags she had dated. She loved how quiet he was, his shyness seemed cute, he was humble and modest and she loved the quirks that only come from a small-town-country-boy. In turn, Kyle loved her sweetness and definitely loved how beautiful she was, especially the couple times they had sex. But after the first great couple weeks, he started to notice Jules drifting away from him. He tried to ignore the signs at first but toward the end, he had pretty much just been waiting for the final blow. Their conversations became dull, Jules seemed increasingly disinterested in anything Kyle had to say. At the first signs of trouble he tried everything he could to get the fire of their relationship back up to the blaze it had been but all the flowers and kind words in the world wouldn't have been able to rekindle what had dwindled to an almost extinguished match. By the end, Jules hadn't even tried pretending anymore and would usually spend her nights out with Kyle talking to other friends.

On the night of May 26th Kyle received the last text message he would ever get from the beautiful blonde girl named Julie.

"We just aren't right for each other. Sorry. Goodbye."

Kyle's heart sunk even though he knew those words, in some form, were coming. He cursed himself for thinking he could have held onto anything so beautiful, scolded himself for trying. He didn't cry, he quickly started to realize she wasn't worth it. His anger for himself eventually turned outward to Julie and how she had toyed with him just because she wanted something different, if only for a short time.

He opened his phone to call the one person that would listen to his tirade and then offer condolences. Kyle dialed his mother, but she didn't answer.

Three

Something was not right. The last thing Kyle could remember was falling asleep in his parents' bed, it had taken a long time but he must have finally slept. He was no longer in their soft bed. Whatever he was lying on now was rough and poked him, he imagined it to be straw or hay. The air around him reeked terribly, his mind immediately brought up an image of a sun-baked porta-potty. He slowly began opening his eyes. He ached and his movements felt slow, even his eyes were reluctant to obey their commands. He pushed himself up from the material he was lying on and slowly the world around him began to come into focus. As he looked around, his mind tossed up so many questions they just became an incoherent mess and he felt on the verge of panic.

Rising up into a sitting position he noticed that his bed was exactly what he had thought it was; a bale of hay (or something like hay), the rough twine was starting to rot and would soon break. He seemed to be on the back wall of a large, open building like an airplane hangar. It was dark, the only light coming from thin slits high in the other three walls. The light that trickled in was weak and a dull maroon color, like the sunset through the smoke of a forest fire. He could just make out small dark rectangles along the wall randomly. They looked like bales of hay, all in different stages of freshness.

As Kyle continued to scan his sparse, dark surroundings a man's voice spoke from his right, "You're finally awake."

Kyle turned his head with a quick, almost involuntary jerk toward the voice and his neck let out an audible crack resulting in a quick, sharp pain. Rubbing the burning muscles in his neck he noticed a person was walking toward him from the corner to his right. Behind this person was a group of silhouettes that looked like more people sitting both on the dirt floor and on a couple hay bales.

"Whoa easy man. Take it slow, you've been out a while." The person said as they came close enough for the dull, maroon light to illuminate. "Just sit for a minute and I'll explain some things that I'm sure you're wondering about. Though I won't be able to explain much."

Kyle pulled his legs down into a sitting position on the bale. The person that had been speaking sat next to him. He was a short, round man that looked to be in his late thirties. He looked as though, at one point, he had been fairly well dressed and groomed but now his light blue, button-up shirt and black dress pants were dirty and wrinkled. It seemed apparent that he had been wearing those clothes for quite a while and his thinning, dishwater-blond hair, probably at one time combed neatly, looked like the hair of someone who was raised from bed during the middle of the night. Kyle pictured the man as a car salesman on a better day.

"You just take your time. I bet you feel like shit. My name is Ed by the way." The man said brightly as he lightly thumped Kyle on the back like a little league coach consoling a player that just struck out.

Kyle sat silently, scanning the nearly empty expanse of the large building but all he could really make out were the rectangular shapes of hay bales, a dirt floor, and the huddled shapes in the corner.

"I suppose you're wondering where you are. It's what we've all wondered and really I can't answer that question. All I remember…" Ed said as he stared into the dull red emptiness seeming to have just made some connection. "Well, all anyone remembers actually is going to sleep then waking up on a rotting bale of hay in this building." His voice dropped and sounded sad as he recalled the last part. "I've been here the longest but don't ask me how long. There doesn't seem to be any time here, even my Rolex stopped working." He paused and shook his dirty shirt sleeve down to look at his large, silver watch. "I guess I got here at three o'clock." His voice now sounded flat and tired as if the conversation made him remember things he had been trying to ignore. "Oh yeah, if you're wondering about the wonderful odor in here that's the bathroom over there." Ed gestured to the far corner to their left. "Do your best to cover your leavings please." He said with the slightest hint of humor and Kyle saw the ghost of a smile flash across his lips.

With panic and fear bubbling in his bowels, Kyle's confusion thickened to the point that he was sure he was still in some vivid dream. "I have to shit in the corner?!" Kyle suddenly said incredulously, his voice was rough in his throat like he had just gotten over a cold.

Ed jumped just a little at the sudden sound of Kyle's question. "Sorry man."

"What the hell is going on?" Kyle asked even though he was already sure of the answer his new friend was about to give.

"I have no idea." Ed suddenly sounded as serious as a doctor talking to a doomed patient. "Seriously. We all wake up here and then slowly people disappear, when I got here there was probably twenty people here. One by one they disappeared. I have no idea where they went or how. I don't even know where the fucking door is!" Ed's voice rose as he talked till he sounded like he may break into tears at any moment. "With you now, there are five of us and I've been here the longest so I guess I'm next."

Kyle's mind searched what Ed was telling him for any clue or answer as to where he was and why but nothing made any sense. Then a question came to the front of his scurrying thoughts, one he thought to be fairly important; "How do we get food or water?"

"Well....There are two slots that open up over there, one with water and one with some kind of food. It's weird but actually tastes pretty good." Ed pointed to the wall on their right just down from the shapes of the other people. "Oh yeah, I can take you over and introduce you to your roommates."

Ed rose from the bale and offered Kyle a hand to help him stand. Kyle took his hand even though he doubted he needed it and stood up. His head swam and the room wavered in front of him, he grasped tighter to Ed's hand for balance.

"Whoa, stood up too fast," Kyle said as his head settled and he regained his balance.

"No. I think it's some kind of effect of whatever drug they gave us to bring us here."

Slowly letting go of Ed's hand, the two of them walked toward the small group of people in the corner. Kyle's legs felt weak and rubbery and his mind felt clouded but he pushed hard trying to keep his fear from boiling over inside of him.

The dirt floor crunched beneath their feet and Kyle suddenly realized he was barefoot. *Of course, he was wearing the same clothes he had on when he went to sleep,* Kyle thought to himself and he was suddenly happy that he had gone to bed with a t-shirt and sweatpants.

"Everyone, this is…" Ed began to say but paused as he realized the new guy never said his name.

"Hello….I'm Kyle," Kyle said as he scanned the three people sitting in front of him.

"Yes, Kyle," Ed said, his voice was now back to the upbeat and friendly lilt of the car salesman.

Ed pointed first to a large, teenage girl sitting to their left, "Kyle, this is Jillian." Then quickly added, "Not Jill."

Jillian looked at Kyle, her face was large and stern. Her short mouse-brown hair pulled back in a tiny ponytail. Her face seemed shiny and sweaty even in the low light of the building. She didn't even force a smile as she voiced a low 'hello' that sounded like someone fulfilling an unwanted obligation. Jillian had obviously gone to bed wearing pink pajama bottoms that were much too small and a large, white t-shirt that read: Somerset Christian Girls Camp.

Kyle said hello with a quick smile and nod toward Jillian.

To the right of Jillian, Ed introduced Tom, a man that looked to be near Kyle's age. He was thin had short, dark hair and expensive looking wire-rimmed glasses. He rose quickly and held out a hand to Kyle. He stood slightly taller than Kyle and, if it wasn't for his matching plaid pajamas, would have looked right at home in a university lecture hall.

"Hi Kyle, welcome to hell," Tom said as he smiled and held out his hand.

"Hi, Tom," Kyle said as he gave Tom's hand a shake.

"And this is Apollonia," Ed said and pointed to the final person on their right.

Apollonia rose from her hay bale and also offered up her delicate hand to Kyle. She looked as if she was in her early twenties and despite wearing dirty, white running shorts, a dingy, pink tank top and being surrounded by filth she was gorgeous. Kyle stepped toward her and shook her hand but forgot to let go as he stared. She stood just slightly shorter than Kyle, her long, straight, black hair a beautiful contrast to the cream-white of her skin. Her large, bluish-green eyes looked through small, black-rimmed glasses.

"That's an interesting name," Kyle said grinning and still shaking Apollonia's hand.

"Yea it's great," Apollonia said sarcastically with a little laugh. "My friends call me Poe."

"I hope I can call you Poe sometime," Kyle said. He immediately regretted saying something so cheesy to this beautiful girl. In his embarrassment, he released her hand.

With an amused laugh, Apollonia replied, "We will see."

"Well, that's everyone. Nothing else to do here except get to know each other." Ed said and found an open bale to sit down on.

The only one now standing, Kyle took a seat on the closest open bale which happened to be next to Jillian. As he sat on the uncomfortable rectangle she shot him a look of disinterest, to Kyle the look said 'Please don't try talking to me.' And he decided he wouldn't.

As Kyle sat on his bale, around him life in the shadowy building returned to what it had been before his arrival. Conversations went on about movies, books, music, and pretty much anything else that reminded those speaking of home.

Kyle looked around his shadowy prison and he let his thoughts run. He thought a lot about where he was and why then a new thought came to him. A thought that he was surprised hadn't occurred to him sooner, then again his situation was distracting, it was of his parents. Could this be where they were taken? Is there some connection? His brain told him there had to be, it was all too strange not to be related.

"Was there a middle-aged couple here recently?" Kyle asked, interrupting a conversation between Ed, Tom, and Poe about the last time they had ice cream.

"There were a couple different middle-aged couples when I got here," Ed said with a look of concern and confusion, then returned to his previous conversation.

There was no real answer in what Ed had told him but he was sure one of those couples had been his parents and they had disappeared to whatever fate became of those in this building.

Kyle stood up and decided to walk around the area of his new home. Leaving his conversing roommates he walked along the wall and its collection of hay bales. There was nothing that stood out to him except the material the wall was composed of. It was a pale grey that, at first, he took as concrete but its texture was unfamiliar and looked like plastic but felt like stone. Reaching the shorter end wall he followed it until the smell of fetid porta-potty became much stronger. Through the dark shadow of the corner in front of him, he could see small piles of hay that he figured served as toilet paper here and he dreaded the first time he'd have to experience it. He walked diagonally to the next wall and walked back toward the other end where he had awoken only, what felt like, half hour ago. Though he was unsure of how long it had been, like Ed had told him, there didn't seem to be any time here. The low light coming from the small windows high above his head near the arched ceiling hadn't changed at all. As Kyle passed the hay bale that had served as his bed he realized that, also like Ed had told him, there was nothing in the walls that looked like a door. He hadn't even seen any seams.

Touching the solid wall and wondering how anyone got in or out, a sound to Kyle's left distracted him.

"Food's on!" A voice that could only be Ed's said from near where Kyle had left everyone sitting.

Kyle slowly made his way to where he could see everyone's silhouettes grouped. He didn't hurry, he wasn't hungry and the thought of eating anything in this place seemed strange to him.

"Go ahead, it's actually not bad," Tom said, rising from what looked like a trough that had flipped out of the solid wall. In his hands were two greyish looking slabs, it was tough to tell the exact color of some things in the pale maroon light but the objects seemed the color of rotten flesh.

Kyle had the look on his face of someone that has just stepped in dog shit. He walked over to the trough and examined the pile of grey slabs. All the slabs were roughly the size of a really large, thick steak but other than that the association to a steak ended. Kyle picked one of the "steaks" up and studied it like someone studying a small dead animal they found in their basement. The scent was strange and it had the weight and feel of incredibly thick gelatin. The idea of eating this thing disgusted him though he figured the hunger that would soon grow in his belly and perhaps even some curiosity would drive him to take a bite. As for now, he tossed the grey, gelatinous "steak" back into the trough with the rest of them. To the left of the food trough was another trough filled with clean and clear looking water. Kyle walked to the trough of water and an image popped up in his mind. An image he knew well for years in his small hometown.

"Is this some kind of barn? Are we livestock?" Kyle asked the group of people feasting on their grey slabs.

No one answered but the looks on their faces told him that this was not the first time someone asked that question.

"If we are some kind of livestock then what are we being raised for? It can't be for…" Kyle said, mostly to himself. The thought of a barn of people being fed to be used as food seemed crazy but then again pretty much everything since he woke up had seemed crazy.

Kyle left the feeding area feeling nauseous. He returned to the hay bale he had woke up on and laid himself down. The dry stalks of hay (or whatever it was) that composed the bale poked his back and made him itch but from what he saw of the rest of the barn this was probably the most comfortable spot. Lying on his bale his thoughts wandered from his parents to the possibility of being eaten, to wondering where he could possibly be.

The others, having finished their meals, returned to conversations about home. This time, the conversation turned to a subject that came up often, where each had been just before arriving in the barn. Kyle let his thoughts drift away, they were fruitless anyway, and he listened to everyone's tales.

Jillian talked about being at a girl's camp in Washington. She hadn't really gotten along with the rest of the girls and decided to find a secluded spot away from the campfire to set her sleeping bag. Tom had fallen asleep at his home in Bozeman, Montana in front of his television just before he would have gone to bed. Poe had fallen asleep or passed out in bed at her apartment after a terrible, drunken night with her boyfriend. Ed had fallen asleep at his desk at work, he owned a small insurance company and apparently dozed off on a particularly slow day. They all woke up here, on hay bales.

With every new piece of information Kyle became more confused, people from different parts of the country all falling asleep and waking up on hay bales in some kind of "barn". Not to mention the definite possibility of his parents meeting the same fate. The thought of his parents coupled with the thought of the people in the barn being used for food made him feel sick. Down below the sick feeling, the fear, and the confusion was a bubble of hate and anger that was growing like a hot coal in his stomach.

"Hey, Kyle!" The voice of Tom yelled from behind Kyle. "Where were you before you woke up here at Chez Shit-hole?"

Kyle slipped off his bale and shuffled over to the group. Without even sitting down he recounted, "My parents went missing. It was....really strange. Anyway.....I went to their house and the last thing I remember was falling asleep in their bed." Staring at his own dirty, bare feet he paused and thought back on that strange night. "You know....it's really weird, I even made sure the doors were locked."

"They must have broken in.. whoever the hell they are," Ed said matter-of-factly.

"Yea...yea, that's gotta be right," Kyle replied as he thought about that person he saw in the field. "I saw someone....well....some*thing* I guess."

Tom rose from the bale he was seated on as if he was too curious to remain seated. "You saw someone? What do you mean?......where?"

Kyle didn't reply right away. The thought that whoever he saw in the field that night might be the very person that brought everyone here made goosebumps rise on his skin. "My parents.....they live on a dead-end road in the country. There was something in the field that night......I wasn't even really sure what it was I had seen but....." He rubbed his face, "This is just too much. I'm sorry....I'm going to go lay down again."

As Kyle made his way back to his bale, rubbing his head and face the entire time, the small group slowly started conversations again. They talked in hushed voices about Kyle's story and what, if anything, it meant.

After a while, the conversations trailed off and Kyle wondered how much time had passed since he woke up. The barn fell into total silence around him as he thought. Ed was lying on the dirt floor staring up at nothing and the rest looked to be falling asleep on top of hay bales. Kyle searched his memory and tried to estimate the distance to his memory of waking but he found this to be nearly impossible. He couldn't tell if it had been an hour ago or ten. The light coming through the narrow windows still hadn't changed at all. He felt the tiredness he usually felt just before giving in and going to bed but he really didn't know if this feeling was an accurate indicator of time. After an unknown amount of time, he drifted into a disturbed sleep.

When he awoke it was the smell of human waste that hung in the still air that hit him first. His back ached from sleeping on the unforgiving hay and surprisingly his stomach gurgled in anticipation of food. From the ache in his back and the fading memory of many disturbing dreams, Kyle figured he had slept for quite a while. Slowly he rose from his "bed" and stretched. The maroon light outside the barn had still not changed and he figured that it probably never would. To his right came panicked voices. He turned and walked toward the conversation of which he was only able to catch small parts of. By the time he reached Tom, Jillian, and Poe he had heard enough to surmise that Ed had gone missing while they slept.

"You're next, Tom." Jillian was saying as Kyle walked up, her tone almost had a sing-song lilt of teasing.

"Ed's gone?" Kyle questioned the group even though he already knew and was just trying to get in on the conversation.

"Yea, no one saw it, though. We have no idea how they even get in here." Poe told Kyle as Tom glared at Jillian.

"It doesn't matter anyway. Whatever happens outside this place has to better than rotting away on a hay bale." Tom said dejectedly.

"I'll be saved, I'm not worried," Jillian said in her matter-of-fact way of speaking while she clutched a small crucifix hanging around her large neck.

Tom immediately answered, "I'm pretty sure your god doesn't watch over this place."

Jillian stared at Tom as if she were about to say something that would put him in his place but the fear she was hiding had clogged her thoughts and she didn't say a word. Hopelessness hung over the four of them like a funeral veil and the opening of the food trough was a welcome diversion.

Kyle decided he might as well give in and try the disgusting looking "food" they were provided. Food that he now suspected was to fatten them up like Hansel and Gretal. Once again he picked up a grayish slab and hung it in front of his face. It had a slightly sweet, almost mineral smell that actually wasn't terrible but still incredibly strange. Reluctantly he used his teeth to slice off a chunk that he quickly chewed and swallowed. His expectation of ingesting something that would taste like rotten meat was completely wrong. The soft slab had a wonderful, mild taste that was so alien to him that he was unable to even compare it to anything else he'd ever eaten. Eyes closed, he happily finished the entire slab and ended off his meal with a couple of handfuls of what appeared to be and tasted like water.

"See, not bad huh?" Poe said to Kyle as she sipped water from her cupped palms.

"It's weird. Yea, not bad I guess." Kyle said and shot Poe a smile which she returned, her pale pink lips glistening with water. "How do we know this.....this...isn't Ed?" The question fell from his lips, it sounded insane and yet valid.

A look of horror flashed across Poe's face followed by a reaction of disgust. She looked down at her empty hands as if looking for evidence of Ed left there, "Jesus Christ, Kyle, I hope you aren't right...I hadn't thought of that."

"Sorry, it was just a thought. I don't think it would make sense that they would keep us here just to feed us to the next batch..." Kyle offered and Poe answered only with an uneasy smile.

Poe's smile faded into a look of complete seriousness and she asked Kyle a question that caught him off guard, "Do you think we'll ever go home?"

Kyle stared into Poe's beautiful, sad eyes. "No. No, I don't."

Four

"God I hate that shirt, you know that," Poe said disgustedly when she turned to see that her boyfriend, Vince, was throwing on his favorite gothic-crosses-and-skulls shirt.

"Whatever." Was all the response he would offer.

Picking up Virtute, her cat, Poe wondered why she always dated assholes like this. Stroking the cat's soft fur, its droning purr reverberating through her chest, she felt so tired and sad. She grew up hating people like Vince, the type of guys that picked on her endlessly during her early years in high school. Back then she still had a significant layer of "baby fat", huge, ugly glasses, and a gap in her front teeth not yet repaired with braces. It took until nineteen before she really emerged from her chrysalis, growing into her body. Her post high school years were quite a bit different than what she had become accustomed to and she liked it. At first, that is. It only took a year of parties, getting absorbed into the groups that she normally would have avoided in her school hallways, before she realized how truly awful most of these people were. She was young and pretty though so she seemed to always end up surrounded by chest-bumping bros, vapid conversations, and people in general that seemed to have something to prove to everyone. None of this was her, not that she didn't want to party or drink, she just craved a party where she could take a conversation beyond football scores and reality television shows. When it came to dating she had to admit that, after her high school years, she kind of enjoyed getting attention from such good looking men. It just always seemed to end up the same, though; tall, dark, and handsome would turn into vulgar, stupid, and mean.

After placing Virtute down on the bed, Poe did a final assessment in her mirror, she looked good and she knew it. Something within her didn't feel like she deserved to think that as if it betrayed that teenage girl that used to cry into her pillow after school. Dating a tool like Vince betrayed that girl also, she hated herself for ever letting him kiss and touch her.

Deciding she was ready to leave, Poe made her way into her kitchen where it took Vince all the time that it took her to put on her coat and scarf to down an entire bottle of Miller Lite.

Slamming the empty bottle on the kitchen counter he wiped his lips and uttered a guttural burp that seemed to last forever. Throwing his arm around a disgusted Poe he asked, "What d'ya think? Gonna give it up tonight?"

Poe responded only with an obvious rolling of her eyes and a disgusted sigh. She really just wanted to get this night over with.

She knew exactly how her night was going to go; it would be fun at first as they started drinking but it wouldn't be long before Vince went too far. He'd start chatting up other girls, his leers would become blatantly obvious as he swayed, and any criticisms of his behavior would be met with dissidence. Poe would finally end up calling a cab to take him back to his apartment hopefully in time to keep him from getting into a fist-fight with any male within punching distance. She'd hide her embarrassment, utter a couple excuses, a couple apologies before finding her own cab to her apartment.

Possessing the clairvoyance that comes from experience, Poe's night went nearly as she had imagined it would. One of the differences was the fight that she was unable to prevent. They had stumbled out of the crowded bar to find Vince a cab. The person that would soon be at the business end of Vince's fist was in the middle of texting his girlfriend, staring down at his phone when he bumped into Poe. There was no stopping Vince, he was 6'1" and free weights were more of his girlfriend than Poe was. The kid that had only been able to type 'I'm on my w' looked more like a fan of comic books and video games than he was of staring into a gym mirror. Halfway through a sincere and unnecessary apology (he hadn't even bumped Poe that hard) the kid with the unfinished text message was knocked unconscious by a single, clumsy punch. His phone and his head hit the sidewalk hard. The phone shattered into a couple large pieces that ricocheted in different directions, around his head formed a growing pillow of blood.

Poe stood shocked. Her intoxicated brain took a few moments to make the decision to either chase after and reprimand a Vince who was quickly stumbling away or help the poor guy that had the misfortune of meeting her idiot boyfriend. She decided to call an ambulance for the stranger lying in his own blood on the sidewalk. Tears streaming down her pretty face she collected the shattered remains of the cell phone from the sidewalk and waited for the paramedics.

After a teary-eyed talk with medical personnel and a police officer, Poe was able to find her own cab home.

With her apartment building finally in front of her and the cab she just exited trailing wispy white clouds in the cold as it pulled away, Poe pulled her scarf tight around her neck and made her way inside.

Lying on her bed in the fetal position, Virtute pressed up to her back offering purrs of comfort, Poe cried like she hadn't cried in a while. She searched her still drunk mind for where she went wrong, how she ended up where she was. She felt so tired, so exhausted and she was sure she had a stranger's blood on her hands and possibly on her clothing.

After sobbing until she felt there was nothing left, she turned to kiss Virtute and rose from her bed. The difficulty she had navigating from her bedroom to her bathroom told her she had drank more than she thought she had. Once in her bathroom, the face that looked back at her in the medicine cabinet mirror was that of a stranger. The girl staring back looked tired, defeated. Beneath bloodshot eyes were the obvious signs of tears, smeared eyeliner, and the dark bags of tiredness. Not wanting to look into this girl's face any longer than she had to, Poe grabbed her bottle of sleeping pills. She'd had trouble sleeping for as long as she could remember and the pills seemed to help sometimes. Whether subconscious or not she swallowed more pills than the bottle prescribed, if the morning never came she'd be okay with that. She laid herself down on her bed next to Virtute and waited for the sleeping pills to take her.

She was in the deepest reaches of unconsciousness when her bedroom door opened and a thin figure walked silently in.

Five

After a while in the barn, Kyle had gotten into a routine. He counted the days by how many times he had gotten tired and fallen asleep, so far he had counted to five. After Poe's question to him about ever going home, he had used all his free time, which was all the time he wasn't sleeping, running the perimeter (he gave the bathroom corner a wide berth) of the barn and doing a small workout. He had decided that any chance that may arrive that would offer escape would definitely be improved by being in shape. The second day of his workout Poe joined him in his run. They spoke of home as they ran together.

"I hate.... talking.... about my job, it was.... really boring. I had actually.... wanted to be a veterinarian." Poe said between breaths as her bare feet kicked up small, lingering clouds of dust.

"So why.... aren't you?" Kyle asked.

"I just never did it... I always thought.... someday I would. I never... expected that my... life would end in a place like... this."

"Your life... isn't over... yet," Kyle said almost angrily and without breath. "I'd love... to tell you I have... an escape plan.... all ready but.... I don't. Not yet anyway."

"Okay. Well.... let me know when... you do." And Poe laughed just a little laugh. It was the laugh of someone that had no hope for rescues or escapes.

"Did you have.... a girl back home?" Poe suddenly asked.

Kyle wondered if it was an attempt to change the morbid subject or if she was actually interested. With an amused laugh, Kyle responded, "Nope, no girl.... I wasn't exactly... a hit with the ladies. How about you?"

Poe ran in silence for a few moments and Kyle wondered if she didn't want to answer or was thinking of how to answer, either way, when she finally did she said, "There was someone... I had been seeing off and on... More off lately. To tell the truth, he was an asshole."

Kyle decided to leave the subject as it was and for the rest of their run, he just grilled Poe on her musical tastes.

***

Lying on his bale waiting for what would be his sixth sleep, Kyle grinned despite the horrible circumstance he was in. Things were going really well with Poe on their runs and if he didn't think they were cattle waiting for slaughter in some kind of nightmare he would ask her out. He laughed quietly to himself as he thought of the preposterous idea of asking someone on a date in this place. Tired from his running, sleep came easy and Kyle momentarily forgot about his missing parents and the barn.

Sprawled across his bale in a deep sleep Kyle didn't notice a section of wall next to him dissolving like wet sand, white light poured through the opening. He didn't wake up until an arm reached out from the dissolved section and pulled him forcefully in.

He landed hard on a floor that definitely wasn't the dirt floor of the barn. His eyes, still clouded with sleep, were blinded by a bright light. He raised his arm up in front of his face. His eyes seemed to take forever to adjust to the bright, white light. It was a drastic change from the dull maroon light his eyes were used to. His hand that was propping him up wasn't touching the bare dirt of the barn but instead a cold, smooth floor. As his eyes slowly compensated from sleep to bright light, Kyle was aware of someone standing disturbingly close in front of him.

"Welcome brother." A voice said and Kyle assumed that the use of brother to be similar to buddy or dude.

Kyle didn't respond but instead waited for his eyes to fully come around. When they finally did he scanned his new surroundings with horror. Standing directly in front of him was a man dressed in a clean, white outfit that looked to be handmade but made well. He looked a little older than Kyle and about the same height but he looked sickly. The exposed skin on his arms was pulled taught so that his veins and muscle stood out with graphic detail. His face was thin and the shape of his skull was easy to make out, his eyes seemed to bulge from his head. His skin was ghastly pale except for swollen, dark patches beneath both eyes. His hair was the same color as Kyle's dark brown but had a slight wave to it and was grown out, shaggy, and unkempt. In his right hand was something that looked like the severed hand of some unknown beast, shriveled and dark purple with only three, large fingers.

Behind this stranger was a room of horror that immediately made Kyle think of a slaughter house. The bright light of the room seemed to come from the stone walls themselves and with this thought came the stench. It hit him like a fist. The room stunk strongly of death and rotten meat, he found himself wishing for the shit smell of the barn. Gore littered the floor. What looked like random piles of guts sat rotting in lakes of blood whose shores had begun to dry into maroon beaches. Containers overflowed with what looked like shriveled arms and legs, Kyle even thought he could see hair just sticking up over the rim of a stone container. In a far corner was a pile of discarded clothing. Pajamas, underwear, slippers, shoes, socks and next to those was a separate pile of watches, rings, glasses and other miscellaneous things that could normally be found in people's pockets. Lying on top of the pile of clothes Kyle could make out the dirty, button up shirt Ed had been wearing.

"You going to eat me?" Kyle asked as he tried but failed to keep the fear from his voice.

The stranger laughed in a way that made Kyle even more afraid. "You catch on quick, don't you? And to answer your question, not yet."

The sickly looking stranger bent close to Kyle's face. His breath smelled rotten and Kyle saw almost every tooth was missing from his crazy smile. "Mommy and daddy never mentioned me, did they? I didn't think they would."

At the mention of parents, Kyle wanted to grab the stranger and demand he tell him everything he knows but something made him think he didn't have to.

"I know all the questions that are floating around that little head of yours. Where are my parents? Where am I? Who's eating all these people? Everyone that sits where you're sitting wonders many the same things but they never get the answers. I'm making an exception for you, brother."

"Where are my parents? What have you done with them!? I'm not your brother!" Kyle burst at the stranger, the coal in his stomach was starting to warm up again.

64

"I already said that I would tell you! Shut up! The only reason I'm telling you anything is because I want you to know what liars our parents are and because I spent so much time trying to find you!" The stranger said, his voice rising much too quickly with anger. "Our parents left me here in this…this place to be a slave. To bring people back when I sleep."

Kyle stared at the man claiming to be his brother. He was sure he was completely crazy, but something in the man's eyes was hard to miss. Something told Kyle that this crazy, withered man might actually be his brother. He felt sick. His parents had actually talked of their eldest son, Andy, quite often. They had mourned him, there was even a headstone that they would visit from time to time. The story that he had always heard though was that Andy disappeared into the woods when he was only six, not long before Kyle was born. They never found a body so after so much time they presumed him dead. It was shortly after that his parents had him, it also explained why his mother was always so overly protective.

Andy continued his story as he erratically paced the bright room, "I've been here finding people for The Mouth, well that's what I call him I have no idea what his real name is, I just "feel" what it is he wants me to do and he wants people to eat. I don't sleep, if I sleep here I end up back in people-land and when I sleep there I end up here." Bending so that their faces were squished uncomfortably together, his bulging eyes staring deep into Kyle's he began to sound more and more insane, "I tried y'know! I tried for so long to just stay in people-land but you can't stay awake forever! Eventually, you have to sleep and if I fell asleep and ended up back here without a body then The Mouth would get really angry. It hurts so much, the pain in my head."

Nothing was making sense to Kyle and that didn't really surprise him if anyone had ever gotten a glimpse of this shriveled, tired looking person with too much of the whites of his eyes showing they'd have called the nearest mental hospital.

"I've even thought about offing myself, just ending it all." Andy went on while gesticulating with his scrawny arms, "But he's in my head! He's always there! God, I hate this place!"

Watching Andy grow increasingly angry, a thought entered Kyle's mind and along with it a tiny spark of hope so he asked, "What did you do with mom and dad?"

Andy's bulging, crazy eyes grew even more with anger before he laughed. He laughed a long, loud, crazy laugh that echoed in the small room. "I have something special planned for them, something I reserve only for V.I.Ps."

Kyle stood up and found that he felt large and strong standing next to this tired, weak looking person. At the back of the room was a small section that Kyle hadn't seen before, seeing it now almost made him lose his stomach. Body parts and pieces of "meat" hung from the ceiling. One large piece didn't look human, it looked like a portion of torso from someone's demented idea of an angel. The torso had wings coming from its back that looked to be made of webbed flesh and it still had a head with blank eyes that looked like large, black marbles. Kyle regretted standing and swayed a little.

"That stuff you're feeding us…" Kyle asked but was afraid of the coming answer.

"It's builder flesh. I wouldn't waste the good meat on the cattle." Andy replied and walked up, too close, to Kyle. "But I think I've told you enough, I'll come and find you when it's time,"

Andy smiled maniacally and walked just beyond Kyle. He pressed the palm of the severed, three-fingered hand up against the solid wall just behind Kyle and it began to dissolve again. Through the hole, Kyle could see the dim interior of the barn and Andy shoved him violently back through.

By the time Kyle picked himself off the dirt the wall he had just fallen through had closed back up. His mind swam with new information that he didn't know what to do with. Everything seemed so unreal and nightmarish. Brushing the course dirt off his clothes he looked around the still area of the barn, everyone was still fast asleep and it was then that he decided he definitely had to escape.

Kyle had never thought of himself as any kind of genius or hero but he was going to exhaust every cell in his brain coming up with a way to escape. His situation needed some extra consideration since the building holding him captive had no doors and only tiny windows. The hand that Andy had was the key, literally. He decided that getting that hand and the power it held was the only way he'd be free. Then his mind wondered what "free" meant. What would be beyond the walls of the barn? He wondered if death would find him quickly in whatever alien world he found once outside. He decided dying on his own would be better than becoming some monster's dinner.

***

"What's going on?" Poe's voice startled Kyle to the point he almost fell from the bale he was lying on.

"Oh hey, Poe. I didn't hear you get up." Kyle said as he sat up and swiveled to look toward her.

Poe sat next to him and Kyle looked at her pretty face. She smiled as he stared at her.

"What're you thinking about?" Poe asked as if she really wanted to ask 'why are you staring at me?'

Kyle was still thinking about escape but the thought had just entered his mind that he wanted to save her too. That was if there really was any way to save either of them. He decided while she smiled at him waiting for an answer, to make sure she was with him when he made his escape. Looking just beyond Poe at a motionless silhouette sleeping on a hay bale he decided to try and save Tom and Jillian also. Kyle suddenly laughed to himself as he thought about the ideas currently running through his mind. Not only would he escape a door-less prison in some hellish nightmare world but he was also going to save his three fellow prisoners while he was at it.

"What's funny?" Poe asked.

Kyle still didn't answer but continued to stare. He really did think he was falling for this black haired girl. He fell for girls often but he decided that this girl was different, no really. Even in the awful stench and low light of the barn he couldn't believe how pretty she was. They ran every day now and even though they would wash as well as they could with the trough water once everyone had drank, her face was noticeably oily and her dark hair had started to become messy individual strands. None of that mattered to Kyle and he had the sudden urge to close the small space between their faces and kiss her but he was not brave enough for that. Brave enough to plan an escape and rescue but not to try and kiss a beautiful girl.

"It's nothing. Not yet anyway. I want to get us out of here." Smiling at Poe this was as much as Kyle wanted to disclose to her until he had a better idea of what to do and how to do it.

"What!? You're planning an escape?" The smile on Poe's face had turned to a look of surprise and doubt. "All of us?"

"I guess. I don't know how yet but I'll think of something…I hope."

"Well for Tom's sake I'd come up with something soon," Poe said sadly as she looked over at the sleeping form of Tom on his hay bed. "He is a really nice guy. Ed was too."

Suddenly a thought popped up into Kyle's mind. The sudden way it presented itself gave him the mental image of the shining light bulb over his head, like a cartoon. The idea wasn't much but so far it was the best idea he had.

<u>Six</u>

"Don't go very far, we'll be eating soon," Sandi said standing on the edge of a badly weathered deck, her hand resting on her visibly pregnant belly.

A June sun still hung high in the sky and with child-sized fishing pole in hand Andy replied with some indignation (he'd heard this many times before), "I won't!" and he ran off toward the small stream at the bottom of the hill.

Andy didn't catch many fish, there probably weren't many to be caught in the tiny stream anyway, but that didn't keep him from hours of tossing his line into the water with anticipation. It was another warm, clear, beautiful, evening and he'd probably cast his line until he heard his mother calling for him, even then he'd probably hold out until she sounded angry. He'd have his obligatory dinner and then come out again once it got dark to chase lightning bugs. He was only six but he loved the summer and he looked forward to having a brother or sister to share it with, he knew he'd be a great big brother.

After an hour of casting without so much as a bite, he decided that it was due time to try a different fishing spot. The place that he normally fished was a small clearing in his yard, it was easy to get to but he was getting bored of it and feeling a little more adventurous. There had always been a reasonably clear deer-path that ran along the edge of the stream that his parents had forbidden him from taking. They always said that it was dangerous, wet, and filled with hidden holes but he was six now and he felt that he would be fine braving the path. With a quick glance toward his home above him on a small hill, he secured his lure to one of the eyelets on his fishing pole and started down the path.

As Andy walked, the path became more and more overgrown. Reeds and marsh grasses were nearly twice as tall as he was and the stream had disappeared from sight some time ago. His cheap shoes were covered in mud and his steps were pronounced with a "squish" sound as he continued down the swampy trail. He would have turned back but he knew that the damage was done and he'd have to face his parents' anger either way. At this point he really just wanted to see where the trail would come out, it could be the greatest fishing spot ever.

It was his curiosity that kept him walking even after the trail degraded to a narrow strip of water-saturated ground. By the time he neared the end of the trail he was having to part the tall grasses, his feet had disappeared into thick muck, and the sky above him had grown dark and orange. Andy noticed none of these things and the fact that his mother was yelling herself hoarse far from the range of his hearing never crossed his mind. He was close to the end and he could feel it, he dropped his fishing pole long ago as it kept getting caught up in the tall grass.

72

He would just see where this ended then he would head back home, that's it.

Engulfed in grass over twice his height, his pace slowed by mud up to his knees, Andy finally emerged into a small clearing. It was here that his feeling of accomplishment and relief turned quickly to horror. He had somehow not noticed that the sky was mere moments away from going from a dark orange to black. He immediately started balling, he'd run back toward his home but looking at the impossibly tall grass around him he had no idea which direction to run. He knew his mother would be worried, his father livid. He screamed for his mother, he was so frightened. How could he have lost track of time and where he was so thoroughly? Could they even hear him?

Still sitting in the small clearing he had discovered, the night consumed him with no moon and no stars just absolute darkness. Andy cried and screamed into the dark until his voice finally gave out. He was more frightened than he had ever been in his short life, it was so dark and so quiet. Even the usual sound of the frogs and crickets was absent. Wet and freezing cold he curled up on a patch of flattened grass, pulled his knees to his chest, and sobbed. He missed his mother and father and he wondered if he'd ever see them again.

***

With no memory of falling asleep, Andy awoke to the feeling of being carried and an unfamiliar voice, "You okay little guy? I'm very sorry. My name is Martin...."

With no response, Andy tried to rub the sleep from his eyes and he looked up at the stranger that had just spoken and waked him. The face that his eyes fell upon caused him to involuntarily jump and he found himself immediately wide awake as he fell from the man's arms and landed hard on the ground. The tired, gaunt, almost skull-like face belonged to the man that had been carrying him.

"Come on now, we have a long walk.....get up." The awful man named Martin continued. "My time is almost done here." Offering his boney hand and a rotten-tooth-filled smile he said, "You're my replacement....finally."

Lying on the ground, a sickly-skinny stranger standing over him, Andy first noticed that the sky above him was now a dull, unnatural maroon color. He also noticed that he was no longer surrounded by the tall grass he remembered falling asleep in, the land around him now was barren and empty. A sick and helpless feeling consumed him. He was far from home and he knew it.

***

Andy's parents spent months after his disappearance searching and crying, there had been a lot of crying and Sandi took it the hardest, blaming herself. They eventually found his fishing pole, discarded along a mostly non-existent trail of small shoe prints in the wet soil. Any other sign of where he ended up were long lost in the muck and weeds or covered by animal prints.

By the time Kyle was born, four months later, they had determined that Andy had wandered off and died somewhere deep in the Wisconsin woods. The authorities involved in the search had always been perplexed though by their inability to locate a corpse, even with the help of dogs.

As Kyle grew up as an only child, Sandi kept a tight rein on the boy. She often lied awake at night worrying that some unforeseen harm would come to her second son. About the only times that she ever felt completely comfortable were when he was sitting right in front of her. She didn't like speaking much about Andy but she knew Kyle would have to know about his brother so once in a while she would sit with him and tell stories of Andy. The stories wouldn't last long before she'd retreat to an unoccupied portion of the house to cry.

Kyle almost never heard his father mention Andy, his father was never really one to be open with his emotions, always keeping his "manly" resolve. It didn't matter though because he could see the sadness in his father's eyes. One thought he always remembered running through his mind was that he wished he could have met his brother, he really never thought that he'd one day change his mind and wish he'd never even heard his brother's name.

Seven

Kyle didn't want to tell anyone about the meeting he had with his new brother. He really didn't want Poe to know that it was his own big brother that was going to hack them up and feed them to some "mouth". He also knew that not telling them would make it a little harder to convince anyone that he had somewhat of a plan to escape.

"As far as we know you're next." Kyle was saying to a skeptical Tom as Poe stood listening, Jillian was behind them, near her hay bale praying.

"Yea. Maybe. I still don't understand what you think you're going to do." Tom said in a voice that said he wasn't buying what Kyle was trying to sell.

"Just trust me, please. As far as I can tell I'm the only one that has made any attempt at getting us out of here." Kyle's voice was beginning to rise with frustration.

Tom looked at Kyle and realized he was right. The rest of them were basically just sitting back and waiting for the hammer to come down. With the sound of concession, Tom replied, "Okay. What do I have to do?"

Kyle walked over to a couple of the fresher looking hay bales and slipped off the two loops of twine holding them together. All three of his roommates were standing, watching him curiously. After collecting four loops he tied them all together to form a length of twine about eight feet long.

"You tell me when you're going to sleep and I'm going to tie us together." Kyle tried sounding as serious as he could.

"Why does it seem like you know more than you're letting on?" Tom asked suspiciously.

Ignoring Tom's suspicion, which he also saw in Poe's face, Kyle continued, "And everyone run as fast as you can when I say."

Kyle scanned the faces of his audience for signs of comprehension. He stared at Poe seriously to make sure she understood. She did.

"If you know something that we don't I really think you should tell us," Tom interjected again, the slight anger in his voice increasing with every word. "Why should we just trust you?"

Kyle hesitated and thought about just letting them all know what he now knew but after a moment decided it would only confuse and frighten them more."Please just trust me.

Believe me, I am no hero and I'm not completely sure of my plan but we have to do something. To be completely honest, my plan pretty much ends once we're outside these walls. I have no idea what's out there."

"I still don't know how you plan on getting us beyond these walls but if you do I will be eternally grateful. I suppose if we're killed in the attempt we at least died trying." Tom said genuinely and he walked over and gave Kyle's hand a hearty shake.

Later, no one really knew how much later, when Tom had decided he was ready to sleep, Kyle tied one end of his twine to Tom's wrist. He pulled another hay bale close to Tom's and tied the other end of the twine to his own wrist. There was just enough slack for each of them to do a little rolling around in their sleep.

From the continuous, restless sounds of crackling, dry hay Kyle knew that no one was falling asleep easily. He wondered how long he'd been lying awake himself. Sleep would come much later after many thoughts of doubt and fear.

***

When Kyle awoke and decided he was sufficiently rested, he still called it morning in his mind, he felt the rough texture of the twine tied to his wrist. Sitting up he was happy to see Tom still open-mouthed and sprawled out on his bale sleeping.

With Tom still sleeping he sat and wondered if he'd be able to do all the things he would have to do to escape. As afraid as he felt he knew that, when the time came, he would do those things or he would be killed and eaten. Those were really the only two choices and only the moment itself (once it arrived) would reveal if he had the constitution to carry out such a plan.

When Tom finally began stirring and looked about to awake, Kyle decided he could remove his twine tether.

"Well, I guess we get another day," Tom said as he untied the twine from his wrist and stretched sleepily. His dark hair was now just perpetually styled in what his mother would have called a 'rat's nest'.

"I guess." Kyle agreed as he slipped the twine off of his wrist and looked over at Poe who was still sleeping. Her long hair draped over the side of her bale. He couldn't help but feel a little disappointed that he wasn't able to put his plan into action. His heart was beating much too fast in his chest. In the silent, still air of the barn, he could hear its thumping in his ears. He knew that each "night" would see him sleeping less and less. It was like knowing that something huge was going to happen, and just not knowing when or how bad it was going to be. He just wanted it to happen. Get it over with and hope his plan worked. Then they could deal with whatever was outside the barn.

***

"You're not going..... to tell me your plan... are you? Or how.... you seem to know something..... the rest of us don't." Poe asked Kyle during their daily workout.

"Sorry, no..... Just trust me that I will do... all I can to get you, us out of here." Kyle responded as he continued to run.

"Ooohh my knight.... in shining armor," Poe said but her tone suggested she was kidding.

Kyle would have blushed at the idea of him being some kind of hero if his cheeks weren't already red from the time spent running around the barn.

During his runs with Poe, Kyle had noticed that the soles of his feet were getting hard with callus, he hardly even noticed the rough dirt and he was getting noticeably less winded. The workouts were definitely helping him feel stronger and better able to carry out the events that may lead to freedom. He liked the feeling of adrenaline, he felt strong and almost looked forward to seeing his emaciated brother again.

***

"Do you honestly think you can get us out of here?" Tom asked as he took his glasses off and set them in a place he felt was safe on the dirt as he prepared to lie down and sleep.

"I don't know. I just feel like I have to, or at least go out with a fight." Kyle responded as he tied the twine around his wrist for the fifth time since coming up with the plan. "Can you sleep with your glasses on?" He asked Tom.

"I suppose so. I've fallen asleep with them on many times. I'm really glad I had them on the last time I fell asleep at home." Tom answered with a little laugh as he grabbed his glasses and placed them back on his face.

Kyle lied down on his own messy pile of straw and stared up at the high ceiling of the barn as he waited for sleep to find him, though he figured it would be a while.

"Good night Kyle," Tom said from his bale not far from Kyle.

Kyle smiled and responded, "Good night Tom." It would be the last time either of them had to sleep on a hay bale.

Kyle and Tom had both found fitful sleep when the wall next to Tom began to quietly fall apart into an opening. A grotesque arm of muscle, bone, and earthworm-like veins reached toward Tom and pulled him violently into the new opening. As

Tom fell through the wall his left arm trailed behind, pulling the tether between him and Kyle taught.

Kyle had been in a fairly light sleep, the only type of sleep he'd had lately, and was alert fairly quickly as he was pulled off of his bale and onto the dirt. He didn't pause, this was the moment he had been playing over and over in his mind. His heart accelerated and he sprang to his feet, simultaneously grabbing the twine pulling on his wrist and slipping it off. He followed his twine tether through the bright opening in the wall.

Suddenly, like before, the faint light of the barn was replaced with the bright glowing walls of the slaughter room. Kyle shut his eyes tight a couple times as if to wake them up and get them to adjust faster.

"What the fuck are you doing!?" Kyle recognized the voice of his brother immediately.

Slowly the slaughter room came into view in front of Kyle. His unexpected presence had bought him a few stunned moments. On the floor directly below him was a confused and disoriented Tom. Only a few feet in front of Tom was Andy, his gaunt face slowly changing from surprise to anger. In Andy's left hand was the shriveled, severed hand he used to open the wall. Behind Andy were two creatures that Kyle had not anticipated and seeing them froze his blood for a brief, stunned moment.

It became horribly apparent to Kyle that the two large creatures behind Andy were the ones responsible for butchering the Mouth's next meals. Each one was paused in the process of simply tearing something apart into large, ragged chunks. Both creatures were spattered in fresh and long-dried blood; their tiny heads pivoted toward the commotion in the room, huge grotesque eyes bulged like a frog's. Their large bodies were hunched over their work but they still stood nearly seven feet tall on short, almost comical, little legs. It was their arms that were far from comical, longer than the total length of their bodies with huge ripples of muscle ending in giant six fingered hands; hands that, at the moment, were tearing one of the creatures with the black eyes and flesh wings into ragged pieces.

Kyle's brain screamed at him as he stood frozen, staring at the blood-covered monsters in the back of the room. Tom's hand grabbing his left leg hard enough to be painful brought him back. He reached down and grabbed Tom's arm just above the elbow and pulled. Tom rose to his feet, still dazed but aware enough to know what had to be done. Kyle suddenly stepped toward Andy, a move he had practiced countless times in his imagination, and without hesitation, punched him in the face as hard as he could. He had never punched anyone in his entire life so, with the teaching of many action films, he simply swung his fist into the side Andy's face. The punch landed much harder than Kyle had anticipated, something in his hand seemed to shift as his knuckles connected with hard skull. Andy was again caught off guard and the hard punch nearly knocked him out. With his left hand, Kyle grabbed the severed hand from Andy's grasp.

Turning past a wide-eyed Tom, Kyle rubbed the palm of the severed hand against the wall they came through. The wall had only begun to dissolve when he jumped through it followed by Tom, both of them taking some of the wall's material with them.

"Run!" Kyle screamed as soon as his feet touched the dirt floor of the barn. To his right, he could see the two girls moving slowly on their bales as they were startled awake.

Kyle started running toward the far wall of the barn, it was the wall he figured had the best chance of opening to the outside and not another room. With a quick backward glance, he decided the two girls weren't moving fast enough for him. Veering back into the barn he ran up and grabbed each girl's wrist pulling them violently to their feet. Once up, the girls saw the urgency and fear in his face and followed his lead.

Tom, sensing where Kyle had started to run, was already standing at the far wall when the rest of the group came to a sliding stop next to him.

"C'mon! C'mon!" Tom yelled as Kyle held out the severed hand.

"What the fuck is that!?" Poe screamed as Kyle rubbed the palm of the severed hand on the wall of the barn.

"This is our door!" Kyle yelled as he pushed Poe through the wall as it started to fall apart.

Kyle waited for Tom and Jillian to disappear through the wall before he turned around briefly to see the two large monsters from the slaughter room bounding toward him. The monsters weren't using their tiny legs but instead, their long, strong arms and they were moving nightmarishly quick. Before Kyle leaped through the open wall he decided they looked like a horrific cross between a giant gorilla and a toad.

Finally beyond the walls of the barn, Kyle found himself in an alien world. He had expected this when he had tried to imagine what would be outside. Poe was already almost a hundred yards away with Tom following close and a poor, struggling Jillian far behind them. Kyle didn't pause to take in the surroundings but sprinted in the direction the rest were running. He caught up with Jillian quickly.

"C'mon! You have to run faster!" Kyle screamed at her as he slowed his pace to match hers.

"I...Can..t.." Jillian cried as she struggled to catch her breath, tears streaming across her face.

Kyle glanced back toward the barn and his racing heart leaped into his throat when he saw how close the two "gorilla toad", butchers were getting.

Looking at Jillian struggling, her face bright red from exertion, sweat and tears mingling on her round cheeks Kyle felt an incredible sadness well within him."I'm sorry." Was all he could say as he quickened his pace to a sprint toward Tom and Poe who were now just distant specks in front of him.

Kyle had never been into sports but, when he wanted, he could be decently fast on his feet and now was definitely one of those times. As his bare feet dug hard into dirt that felt just like the floor of the barn. He looked back over his shoulder hoping to see Jillian catching a second wind or somehow putting some distance between her and their pursuers, but what he saw would be etched forever in his memory. Jillian was hardly even running anymore when the first butcher reached her. The creature hardly paused its lumbering but fast gait as, all within a second, it grabbed Jillian's round waist with one giant hand and her gasping head with the other. With a slight twist and hardly any visible effort, it removed her head with a massive spray of bright red blood. Tossing the limp body to one side and the girl's head to the opposite the butcher regained the chase without falling much behind the other. Kyle felt a horror and sadness as he tried to run a little faster. He hadn't liked the girl but watching her die in such a way made him feel like throwing up or crying and he figured that if he survived he would probably do both. His body poured sweat as he closed in on Poe and Tom, his lungs burned and muscles were screaming for him to stop. He could see now where they were headed. The world around him was rocky, sandy and resembled a treeless desert. Poe and Tom were heading for a rocky mound that rose up steeply and plateaued about thirty feet off the ground. He glanced back one last time to check the progress of the butchers and they were closing in but he still had some space.

When Kyle reached the mound, Poe and Tom were already scrambling up its rocky sides. None of them were experienced rock climbers but when your life depends on something you learn to do things expeditiously.

Kyle tucked the stiff, severed hand into the waistband of his sweatpants and started grabbing anything he could use to climb, he found that his rough, bare feet worked well to scale the steep sides of the mound. The hand he had punched Andy with was swollen and screamed with pain that he tried to ignore as he used it to climb.

Poe had reached the top first and reached down to help pull Tom up. As Tom flailed onto the mound's plateau the butchers surrounded them. Kyle was still only about halfway up the side when one of the butchers grabbed at his legs, only a little luck, and a quick movement upward kept him from its grasp. Faintly aware that Tom and Poe were screaming at him, Kyle concentrated on his climb and fought to keep his limbs from succumbing to panic. When he was just within reach of Tom and Poe's grasp they each grabbed one of his arms.

Momentarily out of reach of the butchers the three took a couple moments to catch their breath.

"Where's......... Jillian?" Tom asked between gasps of air as if just realizing she wasn't right behind Kyle.

Kyle fell to his knees exhausted, dripping sweat and as an answer, he just shook his head solemnly. He wanted to just lie down but he knew that sooner or later those long-armed freaks would find a way to get them off of this mound. Still catching his breath he looked around them. The plateau was about thirty feet around and was uneven and crumbling. Kyle grabbed the largest rock he could find, it was all his racing, tired, frightened mind could come up with. Poe and Tom saw his plan and each looked for their own rocks.

Perched on the edge of the plateau the three of them looked down at the butchers, rocks in hand. The butchers were reaching up and trying to climb the mound but the weight of their massive bodies just kept tearing chunks of rock off. Kyle aimed and flung his rock down at the nearest butcher. The rock crashed hard into the creature's right shoulder. The butcher didn't make a sound but backed off a little making Kyle think that it must have hurt it at least a little. Following Kyle's lead Poe and Tom aimed their rocks at the same butcher and flung as hard as they could. Tom's rock glanced off the butcher's chest but Poe's landed square between its bulging eyes. With a sickening crunch sound like a thick board breaking, the butcher toppled over.

With one monster now motionless and looking to be dead the three were energized to do the same to the final one. Each began grabbing any rock that was nearest to them, aiming and throwing. The lone butcher didn't back down; the large rocks that struck it made a sickening "hammer-into-a-thick-steak" sound and it only seemed to grow angrier. Neither of them was able to get a magic hit like Poe had until Tom found a rock that was nearly at his limit of lifting. Carrying it like a little kid handling a bowling ball he waddled up to the edge of the hill. He swung it a couple times then tossed it like a kid shooting a free-throw shot "granny style". The large rock arced slightly and landed on the butcher's right arm snapping it like a large tree branch. With one arm now limp and useless the butcher turned back toward the distant shape of the barn. It pathetically was only able to manage a limping crawl as it trailed its other long arm behind it. Not seeing their final attacker as much of a threat, Kyle made his way carefully down the side of the mound. Poe and Tom followed soon after. By the time Kyle had reached the bottom of the hill the wounded butcher had only managed to crawl about ten feet. Kyle almost felt a tinge of pity for the creature that, only moments ago, would have ripped his head off like someone opening a bottle of beer.

Kyle picked up the large rock that Tom had thrown to break the butcher's arm with. He was apparently a little stronger than Tom as he lifted the rock shoulder high without too much effort. He carried the rock over to the crawling creature and stood just in front of it.

The tiny head of the creature turned up toward Kyle and it seemed to understand what was about to happen.

At close range, Kyle was easily able to drop the rock strategically between the two bulging eyes at the top of its head. The force of the rock drove the butcher's head a few inches into the reddish-grey dirt and it moved no more. The act gave him no pleasure but he thought about Jillian as he did it. He also thought about his own life which he now figured he could hang on to for a little bit longer.

Finally able to relax his aching muscles Kyle looked around at his newfound freedom. He saw now that the entire world was illuminated by that dull, maroon light as if everything was seen through some dark photo filter. The sky seemed low and almost had a texture to it so he assumed it must be perpetually filled with some kind of thick, stagnant cloud. Looking back toward where they had come from, he could see that the barn from which they had just escaped was actually part of a huge building. Behind the barn, a massive structure rose up with only tiny windows here and there and two large towers that, from this distance, resembled smoke stacks on a factory. In the direction they had been running, about another five hundred yards, the barren land ended at a calm sea. The almost completely stagnant water faded into the dark horizon with pointed, teeth-like mountains rising up on either side. A large, square, windowless building could be seen just on the shore of the sea near them. The air was as still as the air in the barn but instead of smelling like shit and piss had a sharp mineral smell like the smell of a bottle of vitamin supplements. There seemed to be absolutely no trees and only sparse patches of dry, dead looking bushes.

"Holy shit you did it!" Tom exclaimed as he and Poe ran up and embraced Kyle in a hug. "I don't care how you knew what you did, we're out of that fucking place."

"Yea but now what do we do?" Kyle asked as the three of them pulled apart and stared toward that stagnant sea. He then promptly leaned over and vomited everything left in his stomach.

Eight

Kyle sat with his back resting uncomfortably against the rocky mound that had saved his life. He needed to rest after what had just happened, well they all needed to rest. The ground was unforgiving and all three of them began thinking the same thoughts about where they were going to hide and sleep. There would be no cover of night but at least the warm temperature of this world was decently comfortable and they knew they weren't going to freeze to death.

"Okay, so how the hell did you do all that?" Tom finally asked after sitting next to Kyle and Poe for what had seemed like quite awhile. "You did know more than you had let on, not that I'm not grateful but you really should let us know how the fuck you knew what to do. And where the fuck you got that...magic glove, or whatever it is."

With the sigh of someone being asked a question they were hoping wouldn't be asked, Kyle responded, "I'm sorry. I'll tell you but right now I think we should get moving again. And trust me, this is as far as my knowledge extends."

Tom huffed with frustration and after a moment asked, "Then where the hell do you think we should 'move on' to? What about that place down there? You can use your magic glove again."

94

Kyle looked toward the dark, motionless waters not far from them and the building that stood on the shore. "I don't know.....I think we should get a little farther from that place." He answered with a motion toward the large building above them from which they just ran from. Standing between that building and the glassy sea his mind filled with thoughts of his parents, of shelter, of more monsters, of death. For some reason, he had a feeling that his brother wouldn't come looking for them personally but he definitely would be sending more creatures and probably would be soon. "They'll be coming soon, I say we just start walking away from here. We can figure things out as we go. The farther we can get the better." Kyle said as he rose to his feet and brushed off loose dirt from his horribly dirty sweatpants. When no one offered a differing plan the three of them started to walk away from the barn and the shore and into a landscape of rolling, rocky hills.

Poe walked up next to Kyle and wrapped her arm around his. "Thanks for getting us out of there. I was pretty sure we were just going to die there."

"Yea but now we're going to die out here," Kyle said morbidly though he couldn't help the tingly, excited feeling that was flitting across his skin.

"We'll figure something out." Poe shot Kyle a sweet smile that finally brought goose bumps to his filthy skin.

After walking for what felt like a mile, possibly a little more, the three dirty refugees crested a rocky hill and stopped. Below them, at the base of the small hill they were standing on, was a flat, sandy valley dotted with various buildings. None of the ten or so buildings were exactly the same and they all ranged in size and shape despite the fact that they all looked to be built with the same material as the barn and the windowless building next to the sea. The buildings ranged from as small as a walk-in closet to as big as a large farmhouse and their shapes went from a plain cube to dome to twisting spiral. Almost all of the structures had some kind of window that must be to let in some of the dim, natural light.

"What the hell is this?" Tom asked as he stood staring with the rest of them at the collection of reddish-grey structures.

"It must be homes. I'm not sure if we want to know who lives in them, though." Kyle answered feebly as he watched for any movement among the buildings.

"We could really use one of those places, though," Poe added and she tapped the severed hand Kyle had tucked in his waistband.

Kyle nodded and started down the slope of the hill toward the houses. "You're right we should at least check it out."

"Fucking great. We're in some alien world full of monsters, let's just go knocking on some doors and see who answers." Tom said, mostly to himself, as Poe and Kyle quickly descended the slope. "I thought we were trying to get away from buildings. Fucking great."

At the bottom of the hill, just on the edge of where the buildings began to rise from the sandy dirt, they watched and listened for signs of life. The dirt around the buildings was marked with footprints that clearly spoke of some kind of inhabitants.

Kyle walked cautiously between the first two buildings, Poe and Tom trailing behind him. There seemed to be no monsters looming in the shadows so he continued toward the center of the little community. In the center of the buildings was a small clear area where Kyle could see something moving.

Kyle waved to Poe and Tom behind him to be quiet and he pointed toward the small clearing in front of them. The three of them peered from the side of a small building that bordered the center of the clearing. A creature was sitting in the dirt and appeared to be playing, it looked like a giant, grotesque version of a human baby. Had it been standing it would have probably been five feet tall, it was fat and round with tough looking, dark purple skin. It was placing its three-fingered right hand into the dirt. Kyle looked at the creature's hands and absent mindedly placed his own hand on the shriveled mass in his waistband.

"It's a builder," Kyle whispered to himself. His mind had been putting the pieces of what he had seen of this world together.

As they watched the young builder playing in the dirt, Kyle understood where the hand he had used to escape with had come from. As the creature raised its right hand from the dirt a small wall followed up with it. The dirt rose into perfectly formed walls until the builder lifted its three fingers and broke contact. Always using its right hand, the builder gleefully tried building tiny versions of the buildings around it. It seemed to be doing well but it had a tough time completing one of the small structures, the walls never seemed to meet in the right places. Placing the fingers of both hands on one of its failed builds the structure dissolved back into dirt. The three watched curiously as the "little" builder tried different sizes and shapes of small buildings until finally giving up. The chubby, dark purple creature picked itself up with much effort and walked slowly toward one of the larger buildings on the edge of the clearing. Its resemblance to some kind of nightmare baby was creepy. It rubbed its left hand on the wall of the large building and disappeared into the dissolved opening.

"Holy shit! This place is nuts!" Tom said once the young builder was gone.

"That's what we were eating in the barn," Kyle informed them as he started across the clearing where the builder had just been playing. Poe and Tom followed close behind.

"What? That meat stuff came from one of those things?" Poe asked incredulously. "How do you know that? That's where that gross severed hand is from too, isn't it? How did you know how to use that?"

"That's not important right now." Was all the answer Kyle was going to give them, at least for now and he swore he could feel Tom's gaze on the back of his head. "Let's just look for an empty one of these."

"Jesus! Be careful which one you open." Tom warned sounding slightly worried. "And I swear to fucking god you are going to tell us more of what you know or......well....I don't know, you just need to tell us. I hate this 'I'll tell you later' bullshit." He added as his wariness turned to anger again.

"What about that one?" Kyle pointed toward a smaller, dome-shaped building that looked like it had been standing for quite some time. The loose dirt around it was untouched by any recent looking footprints and some of the dry, dead looking bushes had grown up around its base.

The three of them cautiously approached the building. As Poe and Tom held back, Kyle took the severed hand from his waistband and hesitantly rubbed its palm on the building. After the second or two, it took for the wall to crumble, a small opening yawned in front of him. Stepping through the hole and into the dome, the wall quickly solidified behind him.

Poe's eyes were wide with terror and worry in the moments that Kyle was in the building. Seconds seemed to last for hours and beads of sweat began to form on both hers and Tom's foreheads. She knew that if something had been in there it would surely have killed him by now, she and Tom would be alone and without that magic hand. Thankfully the wall opened again and Kyle stepped out, smiling and unharmed.

"It's empty!" Kyle exclaimed.

As Poe smiled at Kyle's return she began to walk toward their new, temporary home but something new on the opposite side of the dome caught her eye. As she walked around the building she discovered that her eyes had been correct; there were two rows of some kind of plant growing not far from the dome. The plants were tall, and dark brown but still seemed to be alive and the neat rows they were planted in suggested a small garden. She walked up to the plants and found football sized fruits hiding in the dense, leathery leaves.

"Holy shit!" Tom exclaimed as he and Kyle walked up behind Poe to see what she had found.

Poe grasped one of the large, black fruits and pulled it from the plant. "It's some kind of fruit I think. They must eat it."

Turning the fruit over in her hands, Poe could feel that the black outside seemed to be a thick, tough skin. It felt, to her, like how she imagined the skin of an alligator would feel.

"I think we need to peel it," Poe said as she turned toward Kyle and handed him the shiny, black fruit.

Kyle gave the fruit the same inspection that Poe had. It didn't look appetizing but he knew that they would soon need food if they were going to survive any length of time. Kyle looked around at the ground until he found a large rock that pleased him. He bent over the sharp looking stone and started rubbing the fruit on it, using the stone like a saw (he had seen shows where people opened coconuts in a similar fashion). Leaving black shavings on the rock, the fruit's tough skin began to separate and split. Still kneeling, Kyle peeled apart the small tear he had made in the black skin revealing a bright, blood red flesh. He put the opened fruit to his nose and drew in discovering a sweet, flower-like smell.

"This is weird but we have to try it. Otherwise, we'll end up dying of starvation before we can do anything." Kyle said as he plunged his left index finger into the deep red flesh, a slight tinge of pain reminded him of the punch he recently delivered to his brother.

With Poe and Tom watching, the anticipation of what Kyle would soon discover hanging thick in the still air, Kyle put a large red glob of flesh into his mouth. The flavor of the fruit was strong and incredible. Sweet and a just a little sour almost like the most delicious strawberry mixed with some kind of citrus. With a tiny trail of bright red juice flowing down his stubbly chin, Kyle instantly decided that it was the greatest thing he had ever tasted. Without saying a word, and ignoring the pain in his right hand, he excitedly drove both hands into the slit flesh and ripped the fruit wide open. Red juice covered both his hands as he shoved fistfuls of fruit into his mouth.

Poe and Tom watched Kyle's ravenous devouring of the large fruit curiously until they both decided they had to try one of their own. The plants were full of the black fruits so Tom and Poe easily found their own that they started rubbing on nearby rocks. By the time Tom and Poe tried their first bite of the heavenly fruit, Kyle had opened his second and was covered in juice that looked just like blood.

The black husks of six fruits littered the dirt next to the plants they came from when the three had decided they had had their fill, at least for now anyway. Each of them picked another fruit that they could take with them into the domed building that would serve as their hideout. With round fruits in hand, they followed Kyle into the small dome through the opening he created. The interior was as small and bare as they had imagined it probably would be.

"I can't believe we actually found something good in this terrible place," Tom said once everyone was comfortable and safe within the dome. Sitting with his back to the curved wall his right hand rested on the black fruit he had brought in.

"Hopefully, it doesn't poison us or something," Kyle said from his position lying in the middle of the dirt floor with his wounded right hand on his chest.

"I feel fine....considering," Tom said eventually.

Kyle didn't move but quietly agreed, "Yea, me too."

"So. Does anyone have any plans?" Poe asked sitting cross-legged next to Kyle.

Kyle's mind flashed back to the windowless building next to the water. He felt that he needed to find out what was in there even though he knew the dangers. "No plans yet." He told Poe honestly.

Nine

Sleep came easily and undisturbed within the safety of the small, dome building. Kyle began to enjoy lying with Poe as she'd use him as a pillow or for warmth when she felt chill. He wondered often what she thought of him. She seemed to have warmed to him considerably but there was a definite chance that after all, they'd seen and been through, that she was just looking for some comfort. Kyle wanted badly to ask her or to tell her how he was beginning to feel about her but he had scared away more than one girl by telling her of his attraction to them. His fear would mean he'd wait for her to say something. For the time being, he'd enjoy falling asleep next to and waking with the feeling of her body against his.

After three 'nights' since their escape, Kyle began to feel a little afraid of how comfortable they were all becoming with their new home. They all felt pretty safe as they gathered blood fruits for food (the fruit's plentiful juice also seemingly sufficient for hydration) and slept within the confines of their dome. They even had two areas (a "his" and "hers") area meant for use as a bathroom that afforded enough line-of-sight to watch out for any wandering builders in their area. The bathroom areas were a necessity as their digestive systems acclimated to their new and strange diet. Comfortable or not he knew they couldn't stay here forever.

Sitting with his back to the wall of his new home, Kyle drew a small circle absent-mindedly on the dirt floor with his finger, an opening at the top of the dome let in dim, maroon light. Poe leaned against him as she finished another blood fruit. He loved feeling her body against his even if she was becoming slightly filthy. They all were in need of a bath really. No Laundromats here. No hot showers, not even any rain to help wash them. Kyle couldn't have said that he didn't notice how greasy Poe's long hair was becoming or how dirty her clothes were but he honestly didn't care.

"I think we should go down to the water," Kyle said as he drew abstract shapes in the dirt.

Tom, who had been lying on his back, staring up at the top of the dome, sat up and replied, "I could definitely go for a bath. I'm gettin' all itchy."

"Yea me too. I'd kill for some shampoo and conditioner, though." Poe said with a small laugh. Her voice suggested she was a little afraid of leaving the safety of the dome.

"We need to do something and I think enough time has passed for us to venture out and look around a little," Kyle said as he thought of his parents.

"Yea you're right, we're never going to find a way out of this place sitting here eating fruit," Tom said and stood up as if he was ready to leave right away.

Kyle sensed Poe's growing fear at the idea of leaving their dome and placed his arm around her; he didn't really want to admit that he was probably just as scared as she was. "We'll have to keep our eyes peeled for more of those fucking butchers. Or any other monsters this place may have, I don't really think we have to worry about these builders, though. They seem pretty afraid of us."

Tom laughed, "Builders and butchers? We've got names for all these things, don't we? Seems right I suppose. The way those long-armed things were tearing ap…."

"Stop. I don't want to hear what they were doing." Poe interrupted though she was pretty sure what was going on in the room that Tom and Kyle had come running out of.

***

The three of them eventually decided to make a trip to the edge of the water they had seen, in the least, they could wash up and clean their clothes a little. They came up with a plan to keep a watch for anything moving and in the face of any threat they were to regroup at the dome. Without trees or much vegetation at all, they figured their line of sight would remain fairly open for some distance. It just didn't leave them with many places to hide, they just hoped they wouldn't need to hide. In preparation, each of them ate their fill of blood fruit. There was almost no talking and when they had finished, they all stood as Kyle made an opening in the dome's wall.

Standing just outside the dome that had housed them, the three stared toward a large group of builders standing not far from them. Poe surreptitiously grabbed Kyle's left arm and squeezed it hard as if to tell him how scared she was at that moment. With his free right arm, Kyle placed the severed builder hand into the back of his pants, out of view of the large creatures. The builders, all were near eight feet tall and looked like large versions of the young one they had watched, turned toward them. Poe squeezed Kyle's arm harder, to the point that Kyle was sure there would be a bruise once she released. To their relief, the builders looked much more frightened of them and with a sound like a broken, semi's air horn the group of builders ran as quickly (and comically) as their huge bodies would let them. They scattered, each successively disappearing quickly into their own large building.

"I guess you were right, they're not a threat huh?" Tom said as he started walking.

"I guess not. I can't imagine that eating them and cutting off their hands has anything to do with that." Kyle commented thinking about the wrinkled hand he'd used countless times now.

***

It didn't take long for them to come into view of the beach and the large building on the sea's shore. The land they traversed resembled the southwest deserts of their previous land, just without the sun and heat. Their feet now only hurt when they stepped on the sharpest and roughest of stone. Kyle walked in front followed by Poe and Tom. Each of their heads pivoting constantly watching for any signs of movement, any sign of giant babies or creatures with long arms. Thankfully the world around them seemed quiet and dead. Kyle led them across the barren land to the mound that had saved their lives. Beneath that textured, dead sky the three of them looked at the confused mess of footprints made when they killed two of the long-armed creatures they now called butchers. The patches of dirt where the bodies had been lying were now empty and neither of them wanted to begin guessing what could have happened to the dead creatures.

Silently, the three walked away from the rocky mound and toward the stagnant waters of the mysterious sea. Neither of them really wanted to think back on what they had been through or to even look back toward the large building and its smoke stack-like towers. They all just kept hoping they would awake from this nightmare, safe in their beds.

Standing on the rocky beach, Kyle, Tom, and Poe stared out over the still water. With its glassy surface disappearing at the horizon, the calmness of such a large body of water seemed creepy and wrong. To their collective left was the windowless building built with one wall touching the water , they had started calling it the beach house. Kyle looked from the water and stared at the house, his curiosity was becoming a nagging voice urging him on. The old adage about cats and their lethal curiosity sprang to his mind.

Poe dipped one of her feet, the sole nearly black with dirt, into the water. At the same time, Tom pushed his glasses further up onto his nose. He thought he had seen something break the stillness of the water, far out but he swore he could still see ripples.

"It's really warm," Poe said happily as she submerged one foot completely. "Oooohhh it's almost like bath water."

Tom wondered if what he may or may not have seen was worth bringing up. As he stared out over the water nothing broke the surface again, if anything had, to begin with. He decided not to worry anyone, his eyesight wasn't great anyway. Plus he really wanted to wash some of the grime from his itching skin. If he had seen something it was far out and would be no danger to them.

"Well, I suppose each of us can wash up the best we can while the other two keep a watch," Kyle said as he finally pried his gaze from the beach house. "Poe you can go first if you want."

"No peeking," Poe replied with a sly smile. "I'll be quick, I don't really want to go swimming in here."

Tom and Kyle turned their backs to give Poe her privacy and to watch the land above them and back toward the barn for any signs of trouble.

Poe quickly removed her clothes, carefully set down her glasses, grabbed a handful of loose sand to scrub with and plunged into the lukewarm water. The sand was a far cry from the shampoo and soaps she had been used to but it was definitely better than nothing especially since she had no idea how long she had gone without a shower. It felt like an incredibly long time. As she scrubbed she glanced out at the mysterious water she was immersed in. She had only gone as deep as the top of her thighs but she still worried about what could possibly be hiding in the clean looking but dark water. Her feet only felt a rocky bottom and so far nothing had touched her, for that she was grateful. After she had decided that she had accomplished what she could with sand, she emerged naked from the water feeling infinitely better than when she had gone in. With a quick glance to make sure the boys weren't trying to catch a glimpse, she grabbed her clothes to give them a rinse. Once satisfied with the amount of cleaning the sea and its sand could accomplish she wrung out as much water from her clothes as she could and put them back on.

"Okay, someone else's turn," Poe said cheerfully from behind Kyle and Tom.

Kyle turned around and instantly a part of him couldn't help but wish he had seen Poe bathing. Her long black hair was still wet and hung in tangled strands just over her soft shoulders, her clothes, still, damp clung to her body and Kyle thought she looked absolutely gorgeous. There was little beauty in this place so Kyle really couldn't help but stare, mouth open, at the dark-haired girl and her ivory skin.

"What're you looking at Kyle?" Poe asked with a tone that said she didn't actually need an answer.

Kyle composed himself and started toward the water for his turn at cleaning. As he passed Poe she flashed him a smile that made his face flush and burn.

As Kyle finished cleaning in the warm water, the sand working decently well as soap, he put his wet clothes back on. The beach house, not far off, never seemed to leave his peripheral vision, nervous excitement he felt told him that he would end up inside that building before they left.

"Feels pretty good to be, kind of, clean," Poe said to Kyle as they stood on their watch. Behind them came the sounds of Tom hurrying through his cleaning process.

"Huh? Oh, yea it does." Kyle responded as he realized he had been staring at the beach house again. He looked out over the dead landscape for anything he may have missed while distracted. Thankfully, there was nothing.

Tom approached the water. His mind was trying to decide whether his desire to bathe or his fear of what he thought he saw was stronger. Never taking his wide eyes from the expanse of water before him he stood in ankle-deep and quickly splashed himself with some of the water. He rubbed some course sand on his skin, splashed himself again and considered it good enough. He felt immense relief to have his feet out of the water.

"Well, now what? Back to the dome?" Tom asked as he approached Kyle and Poe.

Kyle didn't reply but looked toward the beach house. Poe just looked at Kyle with concern.

"You're going in there aren't you?" Tom asked Kyle.

Kyle turned toward Tom and Poe, took the severed hand from the waistband of his pants, and said, "I have to. What if my parents are in there?"

"If they are they'll be guarded. You have no idea what's in there man." Tom said, his tone rising with concern despite how futile he thought his words would be.

Kyle looked to Poe who looked back at him with a sad understanding. "I just have to look."

Leaving Tom and Poe staring after him, Kyle approached the beach house. It rose up large and silent before him. The walls looked to be the same material as every other building in this world. This one was unique in the fact that it had no windows at all and one wall rose up from the very edge of the water. Kyle placed his own hand on the rough surface of the wall he was about to open and he wondered what the odds were that his parents were on the other side. He knew that the chances of a horrible death or a quick way back to the barn were much more likely but he knew that if he didn't check, the not-knowing would drive him mad.

Taking a last glance back toward Tom and Poe, both hadn't moved at all or changed facial expressions (to Kyle they looked like two people about to witness a car wreck), he smiled the best smile he could force from his face and placed the palm of the three-fingered, severed hand onto the wall.

Taking a deep breath, Kyle plunged into the dark hole in the side of the beach house. Just before the doorway closed up behind him, taking away any available light, he had a sense that he could see the floor moving.

The beach house was as completely dark as the depths of a cave. Kyle immediately decided that it had been a stupid idea to go into a building that he already knew didn't have any windows. He should have known that It would be dark he thought to himself. *Why the hell didn't you bring a flashlight?* He turned and started to raise the severed hand toward where he thought the wall would be, he figured he would come back when he had figured out a way to bring in some light. He stopped just before the severed hand reached the surface of the wall, what he felt on his legs made his blood freeze solid in his veins.

Standing in the pitch dark nothingness that was the interior of the lake house, his body frozen midway to finding the wall in front of him, Kyle could feel things crawling on the skin of his feet and legs. Something, no a million somethings, had crawled over his feet and were making their way into his pant legs. The sensation, coupled with the loss of his sight, was horrific and Kyle felt that he was on the verge of panic. Within seconds the sensation went from his legs up to his chest. Without being able to actually see, his mind flashed up images of what it thought was happening based on what he felt. The current image his mind had was a disgusting mass of worms, like maggots they felt, swarming up his body beneath his clothing. In a panic, Kyle let out a scream that echoed in the tall, cavernous building and he lurched toward where he thought the wall should be with the severed hand held in his outstretched arm. He had been a little off and hadn't been turned all the way around so he hit the wall in front of him at a weird angle that knocked the severed hand from his sweaty palm. By the time the severed hand hit the floor with a quiet, muffled landing, the mass of worms, or whatever they were, had swarmed up to Kyle's chin. Sightless and in the grip of panic, Kyle stretched his neck away from the crawling feeling like a drowning man straining to keep his head above the water. He wanted to scream, not that he thought anyone would hear him, but his lips were shut as tight as he could get them as the mass neared his face. With a feeling of horror he had never felt in his life, Kyle decided that he had made a wrong turn and his time was up. He was about to die and from some mass of worms or bugs because he just had to look into this fucking beach house.

Kyle tried to thrash, tried to wipe the worms from his skin but, to his horror, there were literally too many and he was now covered. He could feel the tiny bodies of millions of wriggling worms over every inch of his body and their weight on him made him imagine that they were thick over him. The image in his panicked, horrified mind now was of just a huge, hill-shaped mass of worms with him buried somewhere deep within. Feeling like someone buried alive by living dirt, Kyle quit fighting and let the worms take over. His heart beat at speeds he didn't think were possible as he felt worms begin to push their way in between his lips, up his nose, in his ears and even into much more intimate orifices.

Thinking death would soon come, Kyle felt as if he were floating within the mass of ever-moving worms. The worms became all he could feel. They flowed over his skin and they seemed to flow into and out of his body from every opening possible. Within the embrace of the worms, the picture in Kyle's mind changed to something that he knew didn't come from his own memory. He understood all at once that the worms weren't just inside him physically but also, somehow, mentally. The image that shown bright and vivid in his mind was of the shore where he had bathed, just before opening the beach house except the rocky, barren landscape was replaced with a lush, colorful one. The water he had bathed in was crystal clear and lapped the shore with small waves. The sky was open and a brilliantly bright red. Colorful plants grew thick around the water, here and there the top of a building rose above the dense growth and where the beach house was now standing was a square hole decorated with what looked like thousands of flowers and other colorful objects. Kyle felt information enter his brain with a feeling like taking a shot of straight liquor feels in the stomach with a slow radiating heat. It was strange but he somehow understood many things about the land he had been thrust into. Some of the information he couldn't understand and trying to access it felt like trying to remember a dream that had already faded from memory.

The mass of worms had no name but Kyle understood that they had been like a god to this world. He understood that the beach house had been built over them by the monster that made its home in the large building on the hill in a feeble attempt at containing the worms. It was also that monster's influence that had weakened the worms and the land itself. Like a memory that had yet to be made, he knew that eventually, this world would crumble to dust; eventually, the land would be completely consumed beyond any repair. The collective conscious of the worms seemed desperate and tired, weak. Images, feelings, memories, buzzed through his mind like thousands of blurry, angry bees.

Kyle was not used to communicating via telepathy but he tried hard to push a question past all the confusion to the front of his thoughts. As the worms took information from him but left him with much more Kyle's brain felt full with thoughts and new information. When the answer to his question came from the worms he knew it. Without fully understanding the answer, Kyle knew that his parents were still alive but that was about all. A small, dim, round room with two silhouettes that could have been people lying on the floor flashed through his thoughts so quickly he wasn't even sure he'd actually seen it.

Once the worms had taken all the information they wanted and left all they thought was necessary they released Kyle and retreated as quickly as they had come with a soft rush sound into the darkness. Kyle fell to the dirt floor as warm liquid trickled from his nose, ears, and eyes, mixed with his sweat and ran down his face. His head spun and hurt worse than he'd ever felt. In a position that looked like a sick dog, Kyle violently vomited what little had been in his stomach.

He waited on all fours for what seemed a long time for his head and stomach to settle enough for him to think about standing. Once he thought he could stand without vomiting again or losing his balance he felt around for the severed hand. In the empty building the hand was fairly easy to find, Kyle grabbed it and stood up. His head swam and he felt on the verge of blacking out, slowly the feeling passed and he found solid footing. With his free left hand stuck out in front of him he shuffled over the dirt floor until he felt the surface of the wall. Quickly, as if he'd have to experience the worms again if he waited too long, he brought the severed hand up and brushed the wall.

Kyle stumbled out of the beach house wall onto the rocky shore and fell to the ground, actually happy to see the dim, maroon light that was now bright to his unadjusted eyes. Still feeling incredibly sick, his curiosity of the beach house now sated, Kyle felt a sudden urge to see Poe, to be next to her again, to make sure she was safe. Kyle sat up and turned toward where he had smiled at her and Tom before disappearing into the beach house but there was no one there. To his horror there was no one in sight, he was completely alone.

<u>Ten</u>

Kyle sat with his back against the beach house. Any confidence or hope he had gained from his heroic breakout from the barn was long gone and now replaced with hopelessness and the bitter taste of failure. He could smell stomach bile on his breath and maroon streaks of blood were dried across his face. His head still hurt from the confusing events in the beach house. He wondered how much of what happened within the darkness of the strange building had actually been real, the soreness he felt from every one of his body's orifices made him think that most of it had been real. His head swam with new ideas and knowledge, it was as if he just suddenly knew things that, when he had woke up this morning, he hadn't. Most of what he knew didn't make any sense to him though and he figured he would soon forget most of it.

Despite all his new knowledge, Kyle's mind couldn't help but keep returning to the thought of Poe. He had failed her and he was sure she was back in the barn now, probably to be used as bait for him or just to restock the mouth's meat that was probably getting low-unless Andy had gone hunting again. Either way, she was gone, Tom was also and Kyle was now alone in this hellish world. He cursed himself for ever going into the stupid beach house and leaving Poe alone. Just so he could be raped by a billion worms. He couldn't save Poe, he couldn't even find his parents and now he would probably give up and die leaning against the beach house. He thought to himself that he should have known, he was no hero, he had trouble just keeping a gym regimen. Within his sadness, hopelessness, and disappointment, Kyle felt the coal of anger growing hot again and he suddenly wanted to kill the man that claimed to be his brother. If he could accomplish anything he decided he would kill Andy. With a glance at the severed hand that saved him once, he decided to make a quick check of their dome. Tom and Poe had no way to get into their little home though so there was little hope he'd find them there. After checking he would make his way back up to the barn and rush into what he figured would be a trap and he would do all he could to kill his brother. He knew that even if he could kill Andy he would never be allowed to leave the barn again, at least not as anything other than a human steak. Killing the person that brought him here would have to suffice, he supposed. He would go out fighting, he decided this was the best he could do at this point.

***

"Is he still alive?" A woman's voice asked.

Kyle couldn't remember falling asleep but the sound of the woman's question had clearly roused him from a fairly deep sleep.

"Yup. He was jus' sleepin'." A man's voice replied sounding incredibly close.

As Kyle's sleep-filled eyes adjusted to sudden waking, the shapes of two people standing not far from where he was propped up against the beach house wall began to become clearer. Straightening his position a little as if he may need to stand and run soon, Kyle tried to hurry the sleepiness from his eyes by rubbing them, flecks of dark, dried blood fell from his face as he did. His heart picked up pace from surprise, fear, and anticipation.

Standing only ten feet from Kyle were two people, not monsters with long arms or giant-purple-baby-looking things but actual people, a large man, and a shorter woman. In a quick wish to himself, Kyle wanted the two people standing in front of him to be Tom and Poe but they definitely weren't. The woman was short and probably in her late forties, she had brown hair that had probably, at one time, been cut short but was now messy and growing out. The man was huge, tall and, if not for a bulging belly, could have been a body builder at one time, he was younger than the woman and had a thin crop of blond hair that looked as if he had cut it himself. Both of them looked rough like they had been living like Kyle had been but for much longer.

"Who are you? Why are you even here?" The short woman asked Kyle with a tone of urgency and authority. Kyle figured friendliness was not one of this woman's strong suits.

The large blond guy added, "You know you shouldn't be sleepin' out in the open like this. An' you have blood all over your face dude. Gross."

After deciding that the strange duo in front of him wasn't about to haul him off to the mouth or attack him, Kyle answered, "My name is Kyle. I escaped from the barn...that building up there... with two other people. Who are you? I didn't know there were other people here."

Without a response, the woman crept closer to Kyle as if to get a better look and assess the danger, if any, he posed to them. Several moments passed as Kyle and the woman studied each other. Kyle noticed a three-fingered hand, much like the one sitting in the dirt next to him, tethered with what looked like twine to her waist. She wore black dress pants that were at least one size too big and cinched with a full looking fanny pack. Beneath a tattered leather jacket, she wore a button-up dress shirt so covered in dirt, blood, and other stains Kyle could only imagine that it had once been white. Still standing in his original position, Kyle looked to the woman's large companion. The blond man looked as rough as the woman, his t-shirt was filthy and, to Kyle, looked like it once had been white with patches of black in the pattern of a Guernsey cow. Around the waist of his shorts hung another three-fingered hand, a bag filled to capacity that looked to be made of shirts tied together, and a large fanny pack.

"I'm guessing you used that hand to escape." The woman finally said and her once defensive stance softened.

Kyle pushed himself up using the wall behind him for support, his head was still swimming and he felt unsteady. "Yea. Did you two escape also?"

"We did. My name is Darla and this is Otto." The woman said as she turned toward her companion. "It's been a long time since we escaped and we didn't survive this long by sleeping out in the open. Otto, help him find his feet and let's get out of here, the sea is rising."

Otto didn't hesitate to fulfill Darla's command and headed toward Kyle, who was only standing because the lake house was holding him up.

"I'm fine!" Kyle exclaimed and the exertion it took made him feel like he could pass out again.

Darla shot Kyle a glance that said 'Yea you look fine, you can't even stand on your own'.

Kyle decided she was right, he didn't feel fine and when he looked toward the water he noticed that it had risen considerably since he had entered the beach house. When Otto put his large arm around him for support, Kyle didn't resist. Carefully, with Otto for support, Kyle bent and picked up his severed hand.

As Otto led Kyle away from the beach house, following Darla, Kyle asked, "Where are we going? Where do you two live?"

"We've a cave not real far from 'ere." Otto responded.

Kyle decided to save anymore talking until he felt a little better. Using Otto to steady his walking they followed Darla away from the beach house and in the general direction of the valley with all the builder homes. Just before they would have been within sight of the clearing where the builders made their home they started following a steep incline of land. The rocky hill they were ascending was part of a large swath of land between the sea and the builders' clearing that rose steeply above them into a number of jagged peaks. A definite path could be seen in the dirt where they walked; it ended just below one of the rocky peaks. As Kyle was about to ask where they would go now he watched as Darla disappeared into a hole in the hill that looked hardly large enough for anyone larger than Otto to fit through.

"It's not as scary as it looks," Otto said as he set Kyle next to the dark hole.

With an unsure look shot back at Otto, Kyle crawled through the small hole.

As Otto squeezed (barely) through the cave opening behind him, Kyle took in the dimly lit interior of the cave. Despite the small opening, the cave opened immediately into a cavernous room, the ceiling marked with a number of natural skylights. A tiny fire, now only glowing embers, had obviously been burning in the center of the room. On her knees, Darla tossed some random pieces of vegetation atop the embers and began blowing the fire back to life. Once lit, the fire cast ghostly flickers and moving shadows across the bare rock. Bent over the fire, still stoking it back to life, Darla's shadow fell across a large pile of random belongings that looked like a miniature version of the pile Kyle had seen in the butcher room.

"C'mere and sit. I'll tell you our story, then you can tell us yours." Darla said as she made herself comfortable next to the fire on a folded blanket; a number of blankets randomly lined the small fire.

Feeling somewhat better, Kyle made his way to the edge of the fire and sat on one of the nicer-looking blankets, Otto folded a large, tattered blanket next to him and sat.

"As I said, we've counted over 300 sleeps since me and Baby Huey there escaped what you called "the barn". I like that…"the barn" really fits." Darla said as Otto rolled his eyes as if her insults were so numerous they ceased to be insulting. "I don't know how long you've been here but I'm sure you've seen that not much changes. It never gets dark out, the temperature is constant and there is little life here. The only thing we've found that changes is the level of the sea. Anyway, my story before all this is pretty simple really, I went to sleep one night in Kansas City, Missouri and woke up here. I don't know what they do to the people in that building and I don't ever want to find out. I saw some anorexic-looking freak opening walls with a severed hand while everyone was sleeping so I took the hand from him and escaped, tweedle-dum followed me."

Otto listened silently, his big face clearly conveying his sadness.

"We ran, found this cave and lived here ever since. I don't actually mind it, I used to live in parks and under highway overpasses, this isn't a whole lot different. There are less monsters here." Darla said and she smiled at what was the closest thing to a joke she would say. "The giant freaks at the bottom of the hill are harmless, as far as I can tell. I just leave them alone. They apparently build things and it's their hands we use to get in and out of places, this you obviously already know."

"I hate it here!" Otto suddenly said. "I miss my wife, I miss my cat, I miss everything."

Otto avoided the gaze of the two people listening to him and stared, instead, into the fire. The orange glint of the fire made the tears running down his large cheeks look like tiny jewels. Wiping his face with the back of his filthy hand, he continued, "I lived in Riva, Maryland. I jus' got married. Took a nap in my backyard and woke up here." He didn't tell them that he no longer really wanted to return home even if he could. Too much time had passed and if his family had moved on he thought that would hurt even more than being trapped in this world. He felt as if these thoughts were selfish but he couldn't help it. In this case, ignorance really was bliss.

The trembling in Otto's voice told Kyle that if there was any more to his story he'd have to hear it later, so he decided to tell his, "I lived in Minnesota. My parents went missing in Wisconsin and when I returned home to, well I'm not sure what I was going to do. I was kind of lost I think. Anyway, I fell asleep in their house and woke up in that barn."

Kyle, once again, decided that admitting that sick fuck, Andy could be his brother wasn't something they needed to know. Not right now anyway.

"I don't know what you found in there but I don't think you should have been in there," Darla said in her matter-of-fact way.

A thought suddenly entered Kyle's brain, he looked toward Darla and asked, "Did you guys see anyone else near the beach house?"

"The beach house?" Darla asked and laughed a hoarse little laugh. "Nope. Only you. I think you were lying there for quite some time."

"You with some others? Seems like ya did mention something about them when we found ya" Otto asked, his tears successfully choked back now and his eyes dry but red.

Kyle, saddened by their answer, looked to Otto and replied, "A man and a woman. They were my friends, we escaped together. They were there when I went in but not when I came out...I..I have no idea how long I was even in there."

"Well, we didn't see them," Darla responded tactlessly.

Kyle figured their answer would be the same but he asked his question anyway, "What about an older couple?..........My parents."

Both Darla and Otto looked equally surprised at Kyle's question.

"Your parents are here too?!" Otto asked incredulously.

Darla softly said, "How the hell?"

Kyle looked from Darla to Otto, he knew they hadn't seen anyone. "They....were brought here before I was. They are here somewhere....still alive."

Otto shot Darla a horrified look as if to say, 'Should we tell him?' The look she returned said, 'You tell him."

Otto looked around the cavern as if to find a quick way to escape the conversation. Not exactly knowing how to say what he felt needed to be said he did his best. "Kyle.......I'm....I'm sorry but they..... well....they take the people from that place and.....and they.... oh god.... they.... eat 'em." He waited for Kyle's reaction and reply like someone waiting to be slapped in the face.

"I know they do," Kyle said quickly. "I know but... well trust me... they're alive... .... somewhere."

"If you say so, man." Otto stared across the fire and studied Kyle for a moment before asking, "Wha' happened in there anyway? In that building? I really wanna know."

The question sent fire through Kyle's brain and he felt nauseous all over again.

"You can tell us later," Darla said with enough of a hint of compassion that Otto glanced at her with the same face he would have if he just watched her head grow wings and fly around the cave.

Rising from her place next to the fire, Darla nearly disappeared into one of the cave's dark corners and when she returned to the weak glow of the fire she was carrying something in each of her hands. She placed the objects next to Kyle, "Wash up and eat, you'll feel better and then you can tell us what you saw in there. I've actually wondered about that place myself but, as I've learned with this place, some things are best left unexplored. I think you've piqued my curiosity, though."

Kyle looked down at the two things that Darla placed in the dirt next to him; it was a whole blood fruit with a clean slit cut in its think skin and half a blood fruit husk filled with water. Without too much thought, he grabbed the blood fruit and started tearing into it.

"The water is from the sea down there so not sure if you want to drink it. I'm guessing you've seen these melon things before." Darla said as Kyle filled his face with fruit, the red juice mixing with the dried blood on his face.

Kyle finished the fruit that filled his mouth then replied, "Yea we found a bunch of these next to an empty builder house we hid in."

Darla laughed so loudly that it echoed throughout the cave, "You lived in one of those things' houses? I'm impressed. That also means that you know the rules of the hands."

"I do," Kyle said as his mind flashed back to the ugly little thing playing in the dirt.

"What happened to you? In that building by the water?" Darla asked again as if it was the only thing she was really interested in hearing.

Kyle stared blankly into the fire as what had happened in the beach house replayed in his mind. The surreal experience felt like the memory of an incredibly realistic nightmare. "I just had to look in there."

Gripped in nightmarish memory, Kyle put his hand on his face and felt the crusty, dried remains of the rivers of blood that once flowed there.

With the blood fruit finished off, Kyle started dipping his hands into the husk of water. He splashed the water over his face and made an attempt to wash off all the dried blood, as he did his thoughts never left the events inside the beach house.

His face dripping with water and mostly cleaned of the blood and juice that had been there, Kyle looked up at Darla and Otto and said, "Worms." The wetness of his face, the ghostly light of the fire, and the look in his eyes made him look nearly insane as he began recounting his time in the beach house. "It was dark. I couldn't see them but there must have been millions, maybe billions. I don't know. They felt like little worms..... Or something like worms, I don't actually know. They…they talked to me, in my head. They told me things and took things from my mind. I know how crazy it sounds…" Kyle looked down at his trembling hands and noticed how dirty and blood-covered they still were. He didn't want to remember how the worms felt in his body and in his mind, like wriggling little fingers touching every inch of him.

For a few moments, an eerie silence filled the cave, Darla and Otto stared at their houseguest with faces filled with horror and curiosity and Kyle just looked down at his dripping palms as he tried to find a way to even describe what he felt while in that place.

"All these worms…they…*entered* me in every way you can imagine."

"Whoa! Wait. You mean they went inside you? Like, in your mouth?" Otto asked incredulously.

Kyle didn't answer right away. The memory of how the worms felt inside him had gripped him for a moment. With a great deal of effort, he pushed the awful memory aside and continued his story with a little laugh, "Oh yea.....they entered my mouth....and every single other opening you can think of." He looked at the two for signs of comprehension and the shock on their faces told him he could keep going, "It was horrific....so...many worms. Just thinking about it now....I can feel them on my skin." He paused and rubbed both his arms as if to wipe away unseen bugs. "So...yea. We had a confusing conversation and they just suddenly...let me go. That's when I came out. God, I felt like shit....I feel better now. Thank you, both of you."

"That's fucked up man....and you're welcome," Otto said as he looked from Kyle and into the fire, a look of shellshock on his big face.

Darla just stared at Kyle. Her face studied him as she turned his story over in her mind. She found herself strangely wanting to run down to the building he called the beach house and jump inside. His story was incredible and she had a desire to experience these psychic worms and feel whatever power they shared with this strange land that was now her home. She knew that the rising sea just beyond the cave entrance would consume that little building soon if it hadn't already and there wouldn't be any way to get in for another ten days or "sleep cycles". She decided that if the desire to enter that building still existed within her by the time the sea receded, she would enter. Deep down she knew the desire, curiosity maybe, would have such a hold on her by then that entering wouldn't even be a question anymore, it would be an obsession.

Kyle, still exhausted from his time with the worms, (whatever "sleep" he may have had while leaning against the beach house hadn't done much good) stretched out onto his back on the rough cave floor and stared up at the ceiling and its dancing shadows. It was no hay bale but he didn't think sleep would elude him much longer, his eyelids already felt like they were filled with rocks. His hands stacked on his chest, he could hear a faint sound that seemed to be somewhere deep in his brain that reminded him of far away radio static. The soft sound lulled him quickly to sleep. A sleep filled with dreams of Poe and Tom's screams as they were torn into human steaks.

Eleven

Waiting for Kyle to emerge from the beach house was taking much too long. Tom and Poe were beginning to believe the worst. It felt like they had been sitting on the beach for hours, their aching eyes watching the open land around them and glancing hopefully toward the beach house from time to time. They had no idea how much time had actually passed but guessing from how tired they both were it had been a long time. They really just wanted to be back in the safety of their little dome. Both of them were beginning to struggle just to keep their eyes open, they both knew that they couldn't sleep out in the open and, with no way in, they couldn't return to the dome.

"We've got to get out of here, I don't think he's coming back out." Tom finally said as he rose from the ground, dusted himself off, and stretched tiredly.

Poe had thought the same thing and, up until hearing what Tom said, had been holding back the sadness and tears that came with thinking Kyle was gone.

Seeing Poe starting to cry Tom said, "Sorry, I just don't want to get caught out here and have to go back to that…that barn."

"It's okay, I just wish he hadn't gone in there," Poe said as she tried to choke back the urge to cry more. "You're right, though, we should get moving."

Tom had never been great in emotional situations and a crying girl actually made him feel uncomfortable. As Poe rose slowly from the ground, wiping tears from her eyes he felt he should do something but instead he just stood frozen. Poe just stared for a few moments at the silent beach house. As she did, Tom pushed his glasses up on his nose and did a quick survey of the land around them for any sign of shelter.

Beneath the dead, maroon sky Poe whispered a silent goodbye to Kyle while wiping the remaining tears from her eyes. She would go with Tom to find shelter but she had little hope now of ever leaving this world. She hadn't completely given up but she now felt that it was a real possibility that she'd either die of thirst or hunger or end up some monster's meal. Turning from the beach house she nodded to Tom and followed him in the same direction of the builders' little village.

Walking back toward where the builders lived, they diverged from their previous path and walked up into the bare, rocky hills that rose up between the water and the flat valley of the builders. They were moving slow and, after a brief boost of adrenaline, started to become much more tired. The ground was becoming much steeper and their tired movements were becoming sloppy and careless. Poe felt her strength fading as she followed Tom around the side of the hill they were on, she was exhausted and didn't notice that Tom had stopped completely where the hill ran into a small but sheer cliff face. She didn't run into Tom with much force but it was just enough to knock him off balance. He flailed for a moment, his eyes wide before he reached out for the nearest thing he could. The nearest thing had been Poe and as he desperately grabbed her arm he pulled them both over the side of the steep hill. They only tumbled a couple times before the hill ended above the water and they fell like lifeless dolls into the calm waters below.

Entering the water brought Poe around slightly though her brain was in panic mode and all her senses were useless from complete disorientation. Like a reflex, her lungs tried to draw in breath but only got water. A spark of thought told her that this was it, she was dying. Grabbing randomly, hopelessly at nothing but dark water, Poe's mind started to descend into an infinite and final darkness. The last sensation she was aware of was the strong grip of a hand on her wrist that she knew must be Tom dragging her to her death.

***

About the time Kyle finally emerged from the beach house covered in blood, Poe was returning to consciousness through violent spasms of vomiting. Water tinged with blood poured from her as she retched on all fours and tears of exertion streamed down her face. Once the vomiting trailed off into a series of dry heaves Poe collapsed onto a dry part of the ground. Her throat ached terribly, her lungs burned with every breath, her whole body seemed to shake from exhaustion but she was alive. Lying on her back she tried to calm her brain and collect what information she had. She remembered falling but that was pretty much about all, the rest of her memory seemed unobtainable like trying to remember a night after drinking way too much.

Above her, the room seemed to taper high up and ended at a large open hole that looked up into that unmistakable maroon sky. Turning on her side, her head swam terribly as she did, she looked at the large cavern she was in. It was a huge room that seemed to be carved out of stone, with nothing except for a large, round pool directly in the center. The carved stone floor had a warmth to it and the walls themselves seemed to be giving off a soft glow of light making this place seem friendly and inviting though Poe didn't trust this feeling. An attempt at standing failed immediately as she fell back to the floor and decided to sit on her ass a while before attempting it again. As she looked around the empty room the chill of her damp clothing started to overcome the warmth of the stone floor and she knew she'd have to get up and look around eventually.

After an unknown but significant amount of time, Poe felt like her brain had stopped spinning and she had the strength to stand, her clothes had dried and thankfully a warmth was beginning to work back into her. Slowly, cautiously she began to walk around the large room and soon found a small opening in the wall, the only opening except for the circle of sky above. The opening descended into the rock with what appeared to be roughly carved steps. Staring down the steps she decided she had no other choice but see where they went. Putting her messy, black hair up into a knotted bun she slowly began down the steps. The narrow corridor went down in a slow arch like the steps in a giant lighthouse. The way was lit by the same glow that seemed to be coming from the very walls. As she descended along the curving wall, the stairs began getting larger; she ran her fingers along the wall to feel the strange but wonderful warmth of the stone.

Unsure of how far she had descended, the spiraling stairs ended at another opening that Poe absent-mindedly went through with absolutely no caution. To her horror, she found herself in the center of a huge, high-ceilinged cavern with about twenty pale, black-eyed creatures staring at her. She spun to take in all of the cavern and found that the staircase she came down was inside a large cone that tapered to the ceiling and sat almost exactly in the center of the large room. Scattered throughout the cavern were pale creatures, most of whom had stopped what they were doing to stare toward the black-haired girl at the entrance to the stairway. The few creatures that hadn't already stopped to stare, one by one, turned to see what everyone was looking at and soon the entire cavern was silent and Poe had more black eyes fixed on her than she dared count.

Poe stood frozen except her eyes which darted from one pale face to the next. The creatures almost had a human shape to them except their jet black eyes, grossly pale skin, and their lack of a nose or mouth. Despite the creatures' inability to express human emotion via facial expression, Poe could still imagine that they were looking at her with curiosity and her fear began to fade a little. Feeling that she could move without the thin creatures attacking her, she slowly began to walk from the stairway cone and their eyes followed her movement.

"It is okay. We will not hurt you dear girl, I promise you." A strange, throaty, male voice said.

Poe turned toward the voice and let out an involuntary noise of shock. Approaching her was one of the pale creatures except this creature had some distinctively human characteristics. He had the pale skin and the same thin body structure but where all the others lacked nose and mouth this one had a sharp, small nose and a grotesquely large mouth with absolutely no teeth and his eyes almost had a little color to them instead of the jet black like the rest.

The creature held out a four-fingered hand and added, "It is okay. My friend pulled you from the waters. It is incredibly dangerous in the sea you know."

Poe couldn't help but stare in horror as the creature continued talking.

"I am kind of like you." The creature added with his throaty and proper way of speaking. When he added an attempt at a sly wink to the end of his sentence, Poe thought she may be sick again.

"What the fuck is going on?" Poe said and was slightly surprised by the anger in her voice.

"Please dear. Follow me, you shall have a sit. I am told you took quite a tumble." The creature said with a motion toward a far wall that seemed to have roughly carved objects that could be chairs and tables.

Poe suddenly decided that she really did want to sit down, in fact, she felt like she really *had* to sit down so she followed the creature's lead. With the pale man-fish in front of her, she noticed, for the first time, that they all had what looked like wings folded against their backs. The wings seemed fleshy and webbed almost like a bat. As they made their way toward the lumps of stone that served as table and chairs, many of the creatures seemed to lose interest and resumed whatever activity they had been doing when Poe had entered the cavern.

The talking creature brought Poe to the warm stone that would be her seat then sat himself down next to her on another stone. Poe turned toward the creature and asked, "So what are you? What is this place? Where is Tom?"

"So full of questions, I understand." The creature said calmly. "Well, the name my father gave me is, Nigel. My father was one like you, well male of course."

Knowing that Nigel meant that his father had been "human", Poe stared at him with horror and disbelief.

"It is true. You are not the first to escape from that horrible place on the hill. My father lived here with me until his death not long ago." Nigel stared down at his hands as he spoke of his father. "I honestly cannot tell you how I came to be..... that is one thing we never discussed. My father taught me to speak as he did and told me stories of the place he came from. If you could not have guessed, I do not really fit in with the rest."

Poe turned back toward the cavern with the large cone at its center and wondered how someone could have sex with one of these creatures if that's how Nigel came to be. How do you even tell the males from the females she wondered as she suppressed a laugh and instead asked, "Did your friend also pull my friend Tom from the water?"

Nigel hesitated, his dark eyes looked sad, then replied, "Yes, but he is not well. You only took in some water and just needed some time on the stone. He had an injury to his head from striking the cliff you fell from. He is in another room, alive but only barely."

A heavy tiredness fell upon Poe. She lost Kyle and now probably Tom and there didn't seem to be any way to ever leave this nightmare world. She was sick of the dead sky, sick of all the rocks, and sick of all the weirdo creatures. She had never wanted to be back in her shitty little Minneapolis apartment so bad, to curl up on her shitty couch with some ice cream and her cat and watch a shitty movie but the realization that she would probably never go home again hit her with a wave of exhaustion.

Noticing her distress, Nigel put his hand on Poe's shoulder and added, "I assure you that you are now safe here. You are in the middle of my peoples' sea."

Reactively, Poe recoiled from Nigel's touch and stood up feeling another strange wave of anger brought on by hopelessness and frustration.

"Please. I am sorry. Here, I will show you to a space that will be yours to stay." Nigel said apologetically and began leading Poe across the expanse of the cavern.

On the opposite side of the expansive room, Poe followed Nigel through a small opening that led into a wide hall with openings along both sides. Once in front of the fifth entry, Nigel motioned toward the one on their left of the hall.

"Thank you, Nigel," Poe said sweetly. On the walk to her new room, she had softened and felt bad for recoiling from Nigel. "My name is Apollonia but please call me Poe."

With a grotesque version of a smile, Nigel replied, "You are very welcome Apollonia. If you need anything further please find me."

Beyond the small opening, Poe followed a short, narrow corridor that opened into a fairly large, circular room with what could be a bed at its center. The "bed" wasn't much but a raised, flat slab of stone with a thick covering of something similar to moss making a decently adequate surface which she promptly laid herself upon. On her back, staring into the faint glow of the stone ceiling with tears welling in her eyes, Poe wondered what she would do next. She would eventually sleep though she had never felt so absolutely alone.

In a room not far from where Poe was beginning to cry, Tom lied still on a similar bed. His chest heaved in slow breaths as a tiny river of blood flowed from the large gash that ran nearly from the top of his head down to his cheek. His eyelids moved as his eyes flitted quickly back and forth as if his mind were trapped in a terrible nightmare.

Twelve

In almost complete darkness, Andy's slight frame stood in front of a small section of wall. Slowly he reached for the severed hand tethered around his small waist, his echoed breaths came in sharp rasps. After a pause, he rubbed the palm of the hand on the wall and as the wall fell away his sickly features were illuminated by dim light from the room he just opened.

"I brought you supper," Andy said as the wall closed with a soft rush behind him. From a makeshift sack, he produced a couple round fruits and a few wet chunks of what could possibly be meat.

"Please let us go." A male voice said softly, it sounded weak and tired.

Andy simply stood above the "food" that he just deposited on the floor of the small, round room. With the little bit of stretched flesh, his face had left it portrayed the look of dismay. "This is how it's supposed to be." He answered.

The room was illuminated by a couple of small, glowing rocks peppered in the walls and the dim, maroon light that came from the two small openings in the round wall high up toward the ceiling. The light was soft and weak, removing the details from the one standing and two sitting occupants of the room. One of the occupants, a woman, was sitting on the floor and turned facing the wall. She sounded to be crying softly.

"Please...." Andy said, approaching the two seated people cautiously. "Let's just eat something. Please."

The woman ceased her crying with a couple harsh sounds and turned slowly from the wall. "I can't do this anymore, Andy. I....just....can't."

As much as he could, Andy didn't just look sad, he looked crushed by the woman's words. With the slightest hint of concern in his dead, bulging eyes, he leaned down toward the pair on the floor. Kneeling in front of them he whispered, "You owe me this."

Suddenly, violently the still of the room was shattered as the woman reached up and slapped Andy across the face hard enough to knock him off balance and send him crashing to his boney ass on the hard floor. "We don't owe you anything!" She said loudly, angrily as fresh tears welled quickly in her eyes. "You are sick! You've become a monster!" Visibly fighting the urge to cry again she looked at Andy with tear-filled, tired eyes. "You aren't our son anymore. How many times do we have to say we're sorry?"

As Andy rubbed a sore patch on his face he picked himself up from the floor and asked his parents a question he had asked countless other times. "Why would you leave me here?"

It was frustration and anger that abruptly ended Sandi's crying, this time, her face had gotten bright red and felt hot. "How many times do we have to tell you? We didn't leave you anywhere." As if trying a new approach with what remained of her first son, she forced her voice into the sweetest, most motherly tone she could muster. "Andy....you disappeared. We had a funeral for you....we....we loved you. You have no idea how much I cried."

Andy paused at what his mother said, he almost looked as if he would believe her this time. After a few moments though his face hardened again and he said, "And still you lie! You had Kyle. I know....I know....I know." His thoughts started to become screwed up, as they often did. He couldn't think straight, he was sure it was because of hearing his parent's lies again. With sudden anger, he turned to his parents, leaned toward them but far enough away to dodge another strike, and screamed. "Eat your fucking food or you will die here!"

As he had done so many other times, Andy turned from his ever weakening parents and walked toward the part of the wall where he had entered. This time, he turned, a sick half-smile on his skeletal face, and said, "I already took care of....your best son...Kyle. I fed him to The fucking Mouth!" Emitting what he thought sounded like a laugh he opened the wall and disappeared through it.

***

After Andy left his parents trapped in their barren room, they cried together, held each other, and screamed in anger and frustration. After an unknown amount of time they were both exhausted by their emotional venting and only sat in an embrace on the floor. They'd sleep if it weren't for the pangs of hunger in their stomachs. Without a word, Jack left Sandi momentarily to retrieve two of the fruits his son kept leaving them, he had actually gotten pretty good at opening them up now. It was all they allowed themselves to eat. The strange looking meat though they only used as entertainment, they would hold contests between each other with the goal of tossing the disgusting chunks out the small windows at the top of their room.

"I don't know what we can do," Jack said standing with his back against the room's rough wall, a fruit husk dripping red in his hands. "We could try overpowering him, take that...hand thing he has. I think that's how he opens the wall."

Sandi looked up at Jack with no emotion, most of her face was red with juice of the fruit she was eating. "He *is* our son. But

I think you're right. I'm....I'm so sick of this place. I'm sick of crying. I just want to go home.

Tossing away what was left of his fruit, Jack walked over and sat next to Sandi. Wrapping his arm around her he said, "Honey......I don't....I don't think we're ever going home. I don't know where we are right now but I don't think we're leaving.

Their room was silent and still, Sandi looked up into Jack's hazel eyes; in the dark of their prison she couldn't see how bloodshot they were. They had cried all they could today and she wanted to tap into one of the only emotions that hadn't been drained completely. Forgetting about the dirt floor and walls that surrounded them, forgetting about the filth of their dungeon, forgetting about the horror of their situation, she ran her fingers through the course, uneven facial hair on the face of her husband of almost forty years. The beginnings of his beard were coming in a salt and pepper mix of dark brown and grey. She didn't mind, though, she had long ago given up her own fight with the silver that was slowly taking over her shoulder-length, light brown hair. She kissed his face hard and felt the sticky filth on both of their skin. Nothing mattered as they enjoyed each other, not the filthiness of their own bodies, not the horror of the strange world that surrounded them or the hopelessness of their situation.

Thirteen

Standing in front of the tiny entrance to the cave in which he had slept for what seemed forever, Kyle stared out at the, now much larger, sea. The calm water reflected the maroon sky making it hard to tell where the sea ended and the sky began; the path he had followed Otto and Darla up was now cut off by water. The builder village, tiny bumps in the sand from where he stood, now sat on the edge of the water.

He felt better than he had in quite a while even though his sleep was filled with vivid dreams that made no sense, even now that he was fully awake. He let his thoughts wander from his strange dreams to Poe and Tom but especially Poe and he wondered if she was still alive. He had originally thought they had been taken back to the barn but something inside himself told him he was wrong. He couldn't explain the feeling, it wasn't just a gut feeling. It was as if someone had told him some important information that he had forgotten the specifics of. He searched his mind for something further but couldn't bring anything up that made any sense.

Still thinking about Poe, Kyle heard a noise behind him that could only be Otto struggling out of the cave. Without turning around, he smiled and offered a greeting, "Good morning Otto."

"Ha, thanks. *Morning*, right." Otto responded as he stood next to Kyle and looked out over the endless water. "This place sucks. No sunset, no sunrise. But I guess it's home now."

Kyle looked up at Otto with slight annoyance and responded, "This isn't home to me. I'm getting out of here even if the only way is death."

"Geez man, that's morbid....I've thought the same, though," Otto said with sadness. "I'm jus' too afraid, man. I don't want to die....don't really wanna live either I suppose." He finished by letting out a loud sigh.

"My parents are here somewhere....in this awful place. I'm not sure I'll be able to find them. Either way, though I want to fucking destroy that building on the hill. I want to kill every motherfucker in there." Kyle said as his anger and sadness began to well up and spill over. He didn't even notice that he was clenching his fists with enough force that his fingernails were drawing blood on his palms.

Otto responded with a little disbelieving laugh then quickly changed the subject, "I can't believe that the building down there by the water is filled with worms. That's gross…and fucked up." He didn't want to talk about death anymore.

Kyle ignored Otto's comment, he was trying to forget about the worms and how different he felt since emerging from the beach house. He did understand Otto's derision, though, he was no hero. Getting (almost) everyone out of the barn was probably more luck than anything else. He would need more than just the foolhardy courage that comes from blind anger to find his parents or punish the ones that brought them to this place.

"Well, I gotta take a piss," Otto said and started down the short length of path behind them.

When Darla crawled out of the cave a moment later she made much less noise than the large Otto. She walked up to the spot that had been occupied by Otto only seconds ago. "How are you feeling?" She asked genuinely.

"Rested," Kyle responded, not taking his eyes from the unremarkable horizon. He could have added 'pissed off' and 'sad' but he didn't really want to talk about it anymore.

"Good. I didn't sleep much last night. I've decided that I want to take you to see someone soon." Darla said as Otto walked up behind her to listen. "This water doesn't last long, once it comes up it goes back down after a day or two. Actually, it completely goes away. Then we have another two or three days to get to the cone and back."

"The cone?" Kyle asked unable to resist his curiosity.

"It's a giant cone made of rock out there in the sea. Without a boat, you can only get there durin' the dry time." Otto said from behind Darla.

"Shut up, Otto. But, yes that's what it is. I have a friend there, he saved my life once." Darla said as she shifted her gaze from Kyle to the maroon nothingness.

Kyle looked at her with a look of wonder, "A person?"

Darla hesitated as if searching for the best response then said, "No. Not a human. You'll just have to see, he's different."

"Yea he is," Otto added as he bent down to squeeze back into the cave.

"Jesus! Shut up." Darla said angrily to Otto and Kyle laughed quietly.

Once Otto was back within the cave, Kyle asked Darla, "What are we going to talk to your friend about?"

Darla thought for a moment and finally answered, "I'm not sure, he's just the only friendly face in this whole damned world. He's also connected to this place, everything here seems connected."

"Well, I guess it will give us something to do," Kyle said with a smirk that Darla met with only a look of disgust. He was
156

actually thinking that this friend might be able to help find his parents or at least provide some kind of information that could aid in his vendetta against that building on the hill.

As Darla started down the path, presumably to go to the "bathroom" (she didn't announce it like Otto), Kyle crawled back into the cave. Darla appeared a few minutes later and Kyle decided he wanted a distraction to get his mind off of the fact that they were just sitting idle, hiding in a cave. After finding a reasonably comfortable spot on the floor he asked, "What is your guys' story anyway? How exactly did you escape?"

Once Darla found her own spot on the cavern floor she decided a little "story time" would be okay, "I arrived in that building before dipshit here. Back then there were quite a few others trapped in that building. I was just as frightened and confused as the rest but I was determined to get the fuck out of there, everyone else seemed liked they had given up already." She paused briefly as Otto grunted himself into a comfortable seated position. "Anyway, I knew there had to be a way in and out of that awful place. So I sat up after everyone else decided it was time to sleep. It took a few nights of sitting up but eventually I saw an opening. It wasn't a door, just...the wall just opened for a second. One by one people were pulled into the wall, through that opening. It was after three people had been taken into the wall that I watched as someone was tossed *out* of the wall."

"That was me," Otto interjected somewhat excitedly.

Darla shot Otto a derisive look and continued her story, "Fuck, yea it was this dumbass. No idea how the hell anyone lugged his fat ass around. Anyway at this point I had been marking down when everyone went to sleep and when someone was taken and it seemed like it was somewhere around every ten days. They were also taking everyone in the order they were deposited. So for two nights....if you can call them *nights* I guess....I kept close to a woman named Elizabeth. She was a bartender from Kansas or some fucking thing, I don't really remember. Anyway, it paid off and I saw that wall break away and open up. I didn't even hesitate, I just jumped through the hole and there was this super creepy looking guy with what I thought was a glove in his hand. He was pretty fucking surprised to see me and it didn't take me long to realize that it wasn't a glove in his hand but a fucking severed hand! It looked like the hand off of some kind of monster. The way he was holding it he had obviously just had it on that patch of wall that opened. I didn't really realize, right away anyway, that it was some kind of...some kind of key but I grabbed it before he had a chance to even think."

Kyle's upper lipped curled slightly with disgust as he thought about the gore filled room where Andy had confronted him.

"I had that hand but when I turned around the wall was shut again, I was fucking trapped. Then, from behind, something hit me...hit me hard. I ran. I ran around that room like a trapped rat. That's when I saw all the blood and bones and shit, it was fucking sick. And it was a fucking monster chasing me...big, long arms and a tiny head." Darla threw her arms up suddenly, "I panicked and threw that hand at the wall where I had come in. I couldn't fucking believe it but where the hand hit the wall a small hole opened up and then closed a second later. So I grabbed that hand again and rubbed it all over the damn wall." Darla paused and looked at Otto whose face suddenly looked solemn. "I couldn't fucking believe it but the wall opened and I jumped back into that holding area. I screamed for everyone to follow me.......they had all been sleeping.....I tried I really did."

"I couldn't sleep. I don't know how anyone could sleep in that terrible place." Otto added quietly, sadly.

After a significant pause, Darla continued, "He's the only one that made it out. There were four other people in there. That long-armed thing had a couple of friends and they ripped those people to pieces as they tried to run.....I think they were all confused, they had just woken up. Otto followed me though and we made it out of that place. We ran and ran and ran until we could barely even see that ugly place. It took us a while, at least a day, to find those fruits, I was pretty sure we were going to die of

159

starvation or thirst. Then we just happened to find this cave as we were doing a little exploring."

"Jesus," Kyle said as just stared into the glow of the tiny fire.

The three of them sat in silence for a while as they all thought about their own stories and how things could have ended much differently. Introspective thoughts about their strange, new lives would last right up until each found sleep later.

***

The next couple "days" were spent eating blood fruit around the small cave fire and sleeping. From time to time the conversation at the fire was of life before waking in the barn. These conversations didn't last long because all three got more and more depressed thinking about the lives they were now missing. Otto especially seemed to take it hard as he talked about his family.

Kyle had also started learning that he could no longer ignore the feeling of change within himself after his encounter with the worms. He found it increasingly hard to sleep on the bare stone floor, not because of the hard, rough nature of the stone but because the physical contact made his head sing. He found that the more contact he made between his own bare skin and the rock the more the static sound in his head turned to something like voices. Ghostlike images also began floating through his brain the longer he contacted the stone, he began to *feel* them as if he were feeling something happening to someone else. At first, this all horrified him but it was like having a scab you couldn't help pick at even though it hurt and bled. Bored in the cave he started placing the palms of his hands on the stone just to make it happen. Slowly he found that if he concentrated and didn't fight the strange sensations he could kind of "tune" the voices and images like bending the rabbit-ears on a snowy television. At the best of his self-training, he was able to bring up a brief mental image of the cone of rock with only its small, volcano-like pinnacle sticking above the water. The effort it took made him feel sick so he stopped and sat near the fire making sure that only the clothed parts of him touched the bare stone. The unintelligible voices subsided but the image of the lonely, stone point remained.

***

Waking for the fourth time since entering the cave, Kyle found himself alone next to the smoldering remains of the fire. After a brief stretch he grabbed a few pieces of blood fruit and crawled out of the dark cave. Otto and Darla were just outside the entrance having a conversation, their voices were hushed and he couldn't catch one word of it as he stood up. Aware of Kyle's presence the conversation halted. Once upright, he noticed that the sea was gone. Completely gone, where there had once been water as far as he could see now looked like a flat desert with small stone hills dotting the landscape.

With a look of astonishment, his mouth hanging open, Kyle said, "It's…it's gone. Where the hell does all that water go?"

"No idea. It comes, it goes." Darla answered with a small laugh. "We have to leave as soon as you're ready. The water will be back in a few days."

"Okay, Okay. Let me grab my luggage." Kyle said and all three laughed, now standing at the top of their hill next to the newly formed desert.

"Actually. What size shoe do you wear?" Darla asked Kyle.

Kyle laughed a little as if her question was a joke. "Wait, you're not serious? Twelve, usually I guess."

"I am serious," Darla said as she bent and crawled into the cave. She returned a minute later holding a clean but ugly pair of white tennis shoes. "Here, they're elevens but they should work."

Amazed, Kyle fit the shoes on his feet. They fit decent enough and felt fine. He felt as if he hadn't worn shoes in months and maybe it had actually been that long. "Where did you get shoes?"

"She went back in," Otto responded from over Kyle's shoulder, his tone was slightly angry like a mother whose child did something naughty.

"I did a little sneaking around a couple times after we escaped. I found a huge pile of stuff they must take off the people they bring here." Darla said.

Immediately, Kyle's mind went back to that room where he had first met Andy. He had noticed a large pile of belongings. He was impressed that Darla would risk going back in just to loot but his calloused feet were thankful.

"I grabbed as much junk as I could. You wouldn't believe some of the stuff I found in that pile." Darla said as she casually removed a shiny, stainless flask from her pocket and took a pull from it. "This is for special occasions" She added with a laugh.

With each of them carrying an old t-shirt full of blood fruit, Otto, Darla, and Kyle started their walk across the desert that had so recently been a sea. The ground was still saturated with water but the course, rocky sand made foot travel fairly easy.

Still within sight of the rocky hill with its small cave, Kyle noticed that the ground at his feet was littered with what looked like tiny bodies. Stopping and putting his heavy load of blood fruits down, he delicately picked up one of the limp creatures. Otto and Darla stopped and watched as Kyle held the tiny thing up in front of his face for closer inspection. To Kyle, it looked like some kind of aquatic spider with too many legs. Whatever it was, it was now dead and there were thousands if not millions of their little bodies scattered where they were walking. Dismissively he tossed the little corpse and picked up his fruits, continuing to follow Otto and Darla.

***

Poe awoke in her little stone chamber and sat on the edge of her "moss" bed. She kneaded the soft, thick growth beneath her, it felt good between her fingers. She felt well rested and took this to mean that she had slept for a long time. With a long stretch she stood and decided she would try and find Nigel and possibly some food; she also wanted to find out how Tom was.

Leaving her room Poe was surprised to find Nigel was waiting for her at the entrance to her chamber.

"I am sure you are hungry. Please follow me." Nigel said simply and immediately started back down the hall toward the large open room where he had first met Poe.

Poe stood staring after Nigel for a few moments as she let the chill coursing through her spine subside. She hoped that it was only a coincidence that he was waiting there to take her to get food. With that thought, Nigel, now almost to the end of the corridor, turned briefly and looked at her. It was a look that could have meant 'what are you waiting for' or he knew what she had just thought. She shuddered again.

Nigel led her to another edge of the large open room where stone slabs serving as tables were covered with a number of strange, dead creatures. Judging by the creatures' anatomy, a few could almost have passed for some kind of fish-mutants, she assumed they had all been collected from the water and they all looked disgusting.

"If this is not to your liking we do have a limited number of these," Nigel said as he pointed to the final stone slab against the wall which had nearly a dozen round objects that all resembled the blood fruit Poe had gotten used to.

Once again Nigel's spot-on intuition made Poe's skin crawl. As she walked over to the slab of fruits she decided that she needed to know if Nigel could somehow know what she was thinking so she allowed a single, simple thought to enter her mind, 'Nigel is a piece of shit. I'm going to kill him.'

As soon as the thought displayed in her mind she turned to look at Nigel but he was only standing behind her with a look of disinterest on his disgusting face. 'Don't let this place drive you nuts, Apollonia.' Poe thought to herself but the voice that spoke it was that of her mother. She really didn't know how much more she could take of this strange world.

"Are all of these blood fruits?" Poe asked Nigel as she studied the fruits. She realized the absurdity of her question just after she spoke it as if there were a supermarket just down the road that sold "blood fruits". There were four with a dark husk, four with a lighter, cream-colored husk, and four with a vibrant green husk.

"Blood fruits?" Nigel responded, confused. "Oh. You must be referring to the darkest of the three. Your blood is red, isn't it? Yes, they are all similar."

Deciding to try something different, Poe picked up one of the green fruits and one of the white ones. She took her meal to one of the empty stone tables and sat down.

"I hope these are to your liking. I will leave you but you can find me around if you find that you need anything further."

'I'm sure I can *find you*.' Poe thought as she started to tear into the cream colored fruit with a sharp shard of rock that she figured had been put on the table for just that purpose.

As Nigel turned to leave, his folded "wings" twitched slightly and Poe asked, "How's Tom?"

Stopping but without turning, Nigel answered simply, "He is unchanged. He is not well." And he continued walking away.

Poe decided that when she finished she would find where they had Tom and check for herself. First, she decided to quell the pangs of hunger in her stomach so she pulled open the crème colored husk. This fruit was similar to the blood fruit but, instead of the blood-like juice, the juice that ran between her fingers looked more like semen and the fruit itself was bright white. Despite the white juice, Poe filled her mouth with the fruit's flesh and found that the taste was dissimilar to the blood one. This one was strikingly sweet but had a certain bite to it that she could only think of as a spiciness. As hungry as she was she didn't care much about the taste and finished the white fruit quickly. The green fruit, despite its awful bitter, sour taste, went down just as quickly and Poe's face had anyone seen it, looked like something out of a horror film with streaks and smudges of white, green, and a mixture of both. Deciding she didn't really care about her appearance much in this place she lifted her tank top up to her face and proceeded to wipe as much of the sticky juices off as she could.

With her belly full, Poe started to walk the circumference of the large room. As she walked she watched the pale creatures (she named them angels even though their wings were much more bat-like) coming and going. It seemed they were all just doing day-to-day type jobs; a few were bringing in more mutant fish-like creatures, a few were cleaning, one even walked by followed by six younger creatures. She couldn't help but find similarities to being in a community back home but then the thought entered her mind that she might think the same thing if she found herself in an ant hill or a bee hive. They couldn't live in this big, hollow rock if they didn't do the things she saw them doing.

"Enjoying our community?" Nigel asked from close behind.

Poe, startled, whirled around to face Nigel. "Um yes. It's nice." She said, visibly shaken.

"Sorry to have frightened you. I seem to have a knack for that." Nigel said kindly.

"It's okay, you just surprised me. For a minute there this place made me think of home." Poe admitted as she looked around at the pale bodies passing. "Who saved me anyway?" She asked as the thought occurred to her.

Nigel smiled awfully and turned silently to his left, toward the open cavern. Just as Poe was about to inquire as to what he was doing, one of the creatures was walking quickly toward them. The creature stopped next to Nigel then turned toward Poe. The creature's black eyes looked into Poe's and she thought they looked like two pools of inky night sky, she even thought she could almost see flecks like stars.

"This is the one that saved you," Nigel said.

"Can you tell him thank you?" Poe asked of Nigel without breaking her gaze with the creature.

"I already have." Nigel answered with hesitation then said, "Can you place your hand on his forehead? It's to show him your thanks."

Hesitantly, slowly, Poe reached out toward the creature's face. The creature bent forward slightly. In her mind she imagined the creature's pallid skin would be slimy or at least clammy but, with her palm on its forehead, she found it to be soft and warm. A slight, electric-like tingle ran through the nerves of her fingers, up her arm, and into her spine. Slowly she removed her hand, she had always thought that her own skin was pale but against this creature's her skin looked dark. Once her hand was removed the creature turned and walked away to return to whatever duty it had been doing.

Turning back toward Nigel, Poe asked, "Where is Tom? I'd like to see him."

"He is in the room one down from the one you were in," Nigel answered and, once again, simply walked away.

Poe found Tom lying in a room and on a bed similar to the one she had in the next room. Standing above a body that could have just been sleeping, she was surprised that he actually looked better than she thought he would. The healing wound on the side of his head looked bad but other than that his skin still held the color of someone very much alive. She wondered to herself if he'd be able to see well, when he woke up, without his glasses.

***

More than halfway from their cave-home to the cone tower and having traveled for quite a while, Darla, Otto, and Kyle were finally stopping to rest. Since the ground they were walking on was still too wet to comfortably sit on, the three climbed onto a large, flat rock. It was here that they each consumed one of their blood fruits. They ate in silence. Kyle stared out at the world around them and at the unchanged sky above them, he wondered what the view could have been before The Mouth. He tried to imagine some kind of birds flying overhead, maybe some animals running around on the damp ground, and possibly trees (strange-looking ones of course).

Once they all finished their fruits, Otto decided he needed a second one just before they were to continue their walk.

"Could I get a little of that flask?" Kyle asked Darla as they reclined on the large rock.

Sitting next to Kyle, Otto laughed and muttered an 'Oh God.'

"Sure thing!" Darla laughed as she removed the shiny flask from her pocket and tossed it to Kyle.

Now leery of the flask's contents, Kyle inspected it, rolling it over in his palm. It was a nice, heavy flask with the initials "AJD" engraved on the front. For a brief moment, he wondered what the person had been like that had owned this flask. With both Darla and Otto watching him with smiles on their faces, he unscrewed the cap and drew in a whiff of the contents. His sinuses immediately burned as if he had just breathed in gasoline and he winced uncontrollably, this reaction caused Otto and Darla to erupt with laughter.

"What the fuck *is* that?!" Kyle asked and couldn't help but laugh a little himself.

When Darla finished laughing, Otto was still roaring, she answered, "I think it's some kind of moonshine. It's terrible but it's all I have in this world. Take a drink, it won't kill you."

With a conscious effort not to smell the nasty stuff, Kyle took a swig from the flask. The warm liquid tasted just as bad as it had smelled and burned all the way from his lips to the pit of his stomach. He knew the awful taste would linger in his mouth for quite a while but he enjoyed, always had, that warm feeling radiating from his belly. Deciding that one drink was enough, he capped the flask and tossed it back to Darla. "Not bad." He lied.

Picking up their things, they all hopped down from the rock to finish their trek. As Kyle's new shoes hit the soft, wet dirt he stumbled forward slightly and stopped himself easily by throwing his arms straight out in front of him. With both his palms planted firmly into the soft ground his mind exploded with images and voices. He could now clearly see the huge, rocky cone that was their destination and he suddenly knew that Poe and Tom were both within. Tom wasn't well. There was also something else, something that made Kyle's stomach churn but he couldn't tell exactly what it was. It was like seeing a quick shadow out of the corner of his eye, indistinct and fleeting.

Otto saw Kyle first, on his hands and knees with a look on his face like someone being electrocuted. By the time Otto was at his side, Kyle collapsed face-first into the ground.

"What's wrong?" Darla asked as she ran to where Otto was helping Kyle to his feet.

"I don't know. He was on his hands and knees and looked like he was in pain, then he just collapsed." Otto said carefully releasing his grip from Kyle who was now standing on his own.

"It's okay you guys, I'm fine," Kyle said rubbing his temples. His legs were a little shaky but he really had rebounded quickly. The contact with the ground was accidental and caught him off guard, he wasn't able to control it.

Darla sensed that Kyle knew what had just happened, "What the hell was that? Let me guess, stuff like this has been happening to you since being in that building by the water?"

Kyle brushed some wet dirt and rocks from his pants and tried to decide how much he wanted to tell them. "Yes.... I see things now whenever I touch the ground. The wet dirt... it... must make a good conduit or something, it's never been this strong."

Darla just stared at Kyle as if what he said made more sense than he thought it did, she was already convinced that everything in this world was strangely connected. She decided to herself that it would be difficult for Kyle to even describe the link he now had with this world so she wouldn't ask anything further. She also thought to herself that she wanted to feel this link for herself and would promptly visit the windowless building on the shore once they returned. Even if it meant being violated by maggots.

As the three continued walking, Kyle felt an incredible yin-yang like combination of feelings within himself. The thought of seeing Poe, alive and well made him almost giddy and his pace had quickened but he also felt cold, black, dread deep in his stomach. He couldn't explain the frightening feeling of something awful but he knew that if the ground told him about Poe then he had to believe that whatever the reason was for the dread it was real. Part of him wanted to plunge his hands into the soft ground again to look for what was so awful but he knew that his control of this new power was not enough.

"Here's the graveyard." Darla suddenly broke their weary silence from just in front of Kyle. "We're over halfway then."

Otto was lumbering a hundred feet behind them. "She say graveyard?" He called out to Kyle.

Kyle turned briefly and yelled, "Yea, she said graveyard."

Otto returned, "Oh good, we're more 'an halfway."

It took a while longer before they had walked the distance from where Darla had seen what she called the graveyard to where Kyle could see why she called it that.

All around them were massive bones. They weren't white like the sun-bleached bones Kyle was used to, these all had an orange-red tint to them. There were piles of them and just single ones sticking high out of the sand, some stood at least thirty feet in the air. Whatever animals these had belonged to had been huge. There was no longer any discernible shape to how the bones lied, Kyle guessed their position had changed with the rising and falling water level. It wasn't until the small group had almost passed completely through the large area of collected bones that he finally saw a skull. At this edge of the bone field the remains were more sparse and widely scattered but right next to where they were walking was the unmistakable shape of a skull. In keeping with the theme of this world it was unlike any skull he had ever seen. The lower jaw was either missing or buried beneath it in the ground and all the upper teeth on the massive face were gone leaving empty sockets big enough that Kyle could have poked his head in. It appeared to have eye sockets that went completely around the head, he had counted seven before they had walked far enough that he removed his gaze from it.

"Pretty cool huh?" Darla said when Kyle finally stopped staring at the skull.

"It's fucking crazy.....this whole place is," Kyle answered with a little laugh. "If I ever get home no one is going to believe me."

"You really think you can get back huh?" Darla asked without even trying to hide her skepticism.

Looking up at Darla's back as they walked, Kyle said, "I have to, Darla.....I have to. I don't know why......I've never been like this before. Trying to be a hero. But.....I don't know....maybe because they took my parents.....maybe because of what happened at the barn." He paused, collecting his thoughts. "Maybe because of Poe."

Darla rolled her eyes to herself then asked her question while feigning as much compassion as she could, "That was the girl you were with.....before going into that building by the water?"

"Yea," Kyle responded quietly, sadly. "I don't know. I just want to do something you know? And for some reason, I feel like I can."

Darla didn't really agree and she actually didn't really care. She actually kind of liked her cave, it was much quieter than beneath an overpass, much warmer too.

With a great distance still between them and the towering cone, its unmistakable shape appeared in front of them as a tiny silhouette on the horizon. The three shuffled on led by Darla followed by an increasingly excited Kyle. Slowly the jagged, stone peak grew in size and detail.

***

"I think we.... made record.... time," Darla said as she stepped up next to Kyle at the base of the huge stone spire they had been traveling to. Otto was still just a large, slow moving object in the distance behind them.

Looking up at the strange looking but impressive stone hill, Kyle asked, "So how do we get in?"

Darla, still trying to slow her breathing, laughed a little and answered by pointing to the absolute peak of the cone.

Fourteen

The more time that passed in her new, strange home, Poe grew more and more comfortable. Aside from the creepy Nigel, she felt safe here and the pale inhabitants were as friendly as they could be without being able to communicate. She spent most of her days swimming in the giant upstairs pool, wandering around watching the pale creatures go about their day, and making sure Tom was comfortable though his condition never really seemed to change. Once, early on, she tried to help some of the creatures with their chores but their clearly negative reactions made her return to a position of the spectator. She even asked Nigel if there was anything she could do to help in payment for being allowed to live among them and he only answered with 'Not at this time.' She wondered when the comfort and safety would become second to her boredom and restlessness. She had come to terms with the idea of one day leaving the pale creatures and their cone sanctuary to wander, probably to her death, in the strange world outside.

***

Naked, Poe floated on her back in the warm water of the pool she had woken next to, strange thoughts and feelings flashed through her mind that she tried hard to ignore (it could just be all the stress lately). She stared into the hole of dull maroon above her and thought morosely about the things that may be happening back home. She wondered how long she'd actually been gone, if anyone still missed her, and what they might be doing right at this moment. She may have felt a little less depressed had she known that, as she floated, Kyle was approaching her new home, but as far as she knew, he died in the beach house. She wasn't really sad anymore about what she thought was Kyle's death, she had given up on ever seeing home again and when her time in this ugly place was up she'd leave unceremoniously. Anyone from her previous life that cared had already mourned her loss, they were probably already beginning to miss her a little less and were getting back to a life as normal as they'd ever known. Poe also didn't believe in any god or religion, though her current situation made her believe that the existence of something more than just what she knew as living was quite possible. The finality of death had always frightened her and she had always had a secret envy of the comfort that religion gave some of her friends and family. To believe that dying delivered you to something better sounded wonderful but religion never felt right to her and she knew that, no matter how hard she tried, she'd just never believe. The fear she once had for the dark nothingness of death was gone now but she did wish she had someone beside her. Unless Tom suddenly awoke, she knew that when her time came she would be making the final journey by herself.

Not wanting to be alone with her thoughts anymore, Poe climbed out of the water and did her best to squeeze the water from her long hair before putting her clothes back on. She made her way back down to the busy cavern below; she had decided that the company of the pale creatures was still better than being alone.

***

"We have to climb this thing?" Kyle asked incredulously staring up at the peak of the rocky cone about 200 feet above.

Darla walked up and felt the rough exterior of the cone as if to point it out to Kyle, "It's not as tough as it looks. It tapers and is really rough so there's little danger of slipping back down."

Kyle hopped onto the side of the cone to test it out, "If you say so. I guess if you and Otto can do it…"

"You're funny. I wish fat ass would keep up…. we should just start without him." Darla said as she and Kyle looked back to check on Otto's progress and they were both surprised to see he actually wasn't far from them now.

Once Otto made it to the foot of the tower next to Kyle and Darla and he was given ample time to catch his breath (and finish off his last fruit), the trio started the slow climb to the hole in the top of the cone.

"I don't... understand how that guy is still.. so big." Kyle said to Darla after taking a quick glance down at the large man struggling to get himself up the side of the cone.

"Hey!" Otto responded, obviously close enough to hear what Kyle had said. "A lot of this is muscle!"

Darla paused just long enough to look down at Otto so that he could hear her laugh skeptically and say, "Sure...sure, Otto, you just keep telling yourself that."

Kyle only stared after Darla and continued his climb, he felt bad that Otto had heard his comment. The man may not be all muscle but Kyle definitely didn't want to be on his bad side. He figured he'd apologize later.

Having done the climb enough times to get good at it, Darla led the way up, she was followed closely by Kyle and much farther down was Otto.

Kyle found that the climb really was easier than it had looked from the ground but he was definitely not a fan of heights, he just kept repeating in his mind 'Don't look down'. The higher they got the more and more he had to try and steel himself from looking down. Once they were about forty feet above where they had been standing, Kyle's palms began to sweat and he really had to concentrate to keep from thinking about the growing distance between him and the safe ground. It also didn't help that each time he grasped the rough rock that composed the cone his mind flashed with images and feeling. The images were mostly nonsense to him but the feeling that kept coursing through him like a mild electric shock was of pure fear. Anxiety filled him as he wondered when he'd finally find out what was causing these feelings of imminent danger. About three-quarters of the way up the side of the cone and close to the wide mouth at its top, sweat drenched every inch of Kyle's body. He had to stop every couple of seconds to wipe his forehead with the back of his hands, his overgrown hair was plastered to his head and his clothes were becoming saturated with the oily sweat of fear. Once he finally, thankfully reached the top of the cone the muscles in his arms and legs were starting to shake uncontrollably and Otto had actually caught up to him. It was only now that he realized that his breathing was so quick and strained that he was probably not far from hyperventilating.

"Jesus, you okay?" Darla asked Kyle from her seated perch on the edge of the large hole in the top of the cone.

"I'm f-fine," Kyle said as he collapsed with his arms curled around the edge of the hole.

"Hahaha, you sweat more than I do!" Otto said as he sat next to Kyle.

Kyle's only response to Otto was a glance that told him he wasn't in the mood for levity. So, without warning, Otto pushed his large frame up and over the edge of the hole and disappeared. His splashing touchdown in the pool below was heard a moment later. Kyle pulled himself up so that he could look down into the interior of the cone. The opening looked down into a large, open room and about forty feet straight down was the large pool that Otto had landed in and was now emerging from. Kyle moaned at the thought of having to jump down into that dark water.

"Can you do it?" Darla asked with the most compassion Kyle had ever heard in her voice.

Amplified by the large, open area he was standing in, Otto's voice boomed from below them, "C'mon you two! Kyle, it's easy!"

"Just try and land feet first and stay straight up and down. Watch me." Darla said as she pushed off the edge of the opening and hit the water with a relatively small splash.

Kyle's stomach churned with fear and exertion and his body was soaked with sweat, he stared down at Darla as she pulled herself out of the pool and motioned for him to make his jump and join them. Telling himself that he really had no choice and he had to jump eventually, he crawled to the edge of the opening and, before he could think about it anymore before he could psyche himself into not jumping, he swung his legs over the edge first and then simply let go. His face contorted with effort, he braced hard for impact. The sound of him hitting the surface of the water at a bad angle echoed loudly in the large chamber and his splash was larger than Otto's.

"Oooohhhh," Otto commented as he and Darla both winced.

Their fears that Kyle may have gotten knocked out when he hit were alleviated when they saw the rippled, distorted shape of his silhouette rising from deep in the water. They watched as his head bobbed to the surface and he drew in a massive breath. They both knelt at the edge of the pool to help pull him out as he slowly paddled over to them.

"You okay man?" Otto asked as he and Darla pulled Kyle from the water.

Kyle crawled on all fours from the edge of the pool and collapsed onto his back, breathing heavily. "I'm fine… I guess." He finally said in between gulps of air. "Are we about done with this crap?" He decided not to even mention the barrage of thoughts and feelings he felt when he hit the water. At one point he was certain that the water wasn't going to let him go.

Darla smiled and answered, "As long as you can handle a flight of stairs."

Relieved by her answer, Kyle laughed a little and asked, "Carry me?"

With a laugh from Otto and while still smiling, Darla said, "Get up, let's go."

The fear that had been growing within Kyle as they climbed had drained and overworked his muscles, as he slowly rose to a standing position he felt weak and exhausted. His mind still sparked randomly from what he had felt in the water, he would have to try harder to learn how to control this curse. With a stretch of his protesting body, he slowly walked over to follow Otto and Darla into the large opening they had just disappeared into. It was the stairwell Darla had mentioned and, with his right hand lightly steadying him on the wall, he started making his way down. Still soaking wet, echoes of his shoes squeaking and sloshing seemed loud in the quiet of the stone around him.

The stone stairs were beginning to get larger when Kyle caught up to Otto and Darla who were both stopped and bent over something in Otto's hand. As Kyle approached the pair he heard Otto comment, "I've seen a bunch."

"What did you find?" Kyle asked as he found a space between Otto and Darla to view what was in Otto's hand.

Otto lifted his large hand slightly to give Kyle a better look at the tiny objects he was holding. Kyle's stomach lurched and he physically gagged but luckily didn't vomit at the sight of the three small, grayish worms wriggling in Otto's palm.

Darla was going to ask Kyle if these worms looked familiar but when she saw how sick and pale he looked, much more so than he even had looked when he came out of the pool, she decided she had her answer.

"Jesus, do you think these are the worms that…that went…in you?" Otto suddenly asked as the memory of Kyle's horrible story came back to him. With a reaction like a little girl with a large spider in her hand, Otto quickly crushed the three worms and started vigorously rubbing his palm on the side of his pants. "Oh God. Oh God. Oh God. Oh God."

Eyes wide, mouth open, and in the midst of a horrible flashback, Kyle suddenly thought he knew what was causing the horrible fear he felt when he touched the ground. He wondered where the rest of the worms were. He wondered if they were after him. He was filled with the urge to find Poe and leave this place as quickly as possible, to run as fast as his exhausted legs would carry him. Then a voice in his head asked a single question,

186

'Where would you run to?' and this time, he couldn't avoid emptying his stomach on the stairs.

"Aw, man c'mon!" Otto exclaimed as he narrowly avoided the stream of bile from Kyle.

"You fucking pussy. Help me grab him." Darla said angrily to Otto as she wedged herself under Kyle's right armpit.

If Otto had a tail it would have been firmly placed between his legs as he easily helped support Kyle down the rest of the spiraling stairs.

Kyle felt the world around him begin to sway and come in and out of focus as Darla tried reassuring him, "Don't worry about the worms here. This place is safe. You are safe here. You need to rest."

Before his world faded to black, Kyle looked upon a large, cavernous room where pale, ghost-like figures floated in his fading vision. A part of him was shutting down for a while but that panicked voice in his head was screaming two words over and over, 'the worms!'

***

When the world finally returned to Kyle he slowly opened his eyes to a dimly-lit cavern ceiling. His stomach was noticeably empty and his mouth was terribly dry with the sour taste of bile still on his tongue. He felt weak and every muscle ached but really he thought he did feel slightly better than he had just before he slipped into unconsciousness, but that really wasn't saying much. Because he was much more comfortable than he had been since the last time he slept in his own bed he took notice of it. He was covered with a thick and soft blanket that seemed to be made of some kind of thick moss, his fingers told him that the bed beneath him was made of the same soft plant. Thinking a little more clearly now, he thought about the worms, the danger they might pose, and whether he actually believed they were in this place. It didn't take much thinking before he finally decided that he could come up with no answers before he got something in his stomach or at least something to wet the desert in his mouth. He decided that he must be fairly safe in this place if he were able to rest for what felt like quite a while, he figured a little longer wouldn't hurt.

***

Poe had wanted to surprise Kyle when he awoke by standing in the opening of his room, she figured she could say something clever but when she finally poked her head in and saw that Kyle's eyes were open she was unable to contain her excitement and relief.

"I thought you were gone!" Poe exclaimed as she ran into Kyle's room and threw her arms around him. She didn't want to cry but feeling him in her arms she was unable to fight the tremble that was growing in her throat.

Sitting up as much as he could with Poe on top of him, Kyle wrapped his arms around her and only said, "Poe" softly as some of the last moisture in his body welled in the corner of his eyes.

They remained in their silent embrace for a long time, the tears that dripped from their cheeks disappearing into the mossy bed. Seeing each other again would still have been wonderful under any other circumstances but here, in this lonely, alien world, it was overwhelming. For those moments they held each other the world beyond the stone walls that surrounded them didn't exist. The ugly, maroon sky, the long-armed monsters, the barn, the worms all didn't exist and the memory of these nightmarish things was put on pause. It wasn't until Darla and Otto entered the chamber, each holding an arm's load of fruits, that Poe released her grip on Kyle.

"Well, you must be feelin' better," Otto said as he released his load of fruit onto the stone floor.

Quickly wiping any traces of tears from his eyes, Kyle responded, "I.... Sorry, I think I kind of lost it there."

Darla dropped her load of fruits next to Otto's much larger load and said, "It's okay. Eat some fruit, you need it. Then I'll introduce you to Nigel." She then motioned to Otto and they both left the room.

"Here I'll get you one," Poe said as Kyle moved to grab one of the many fruits piled on his floor. "You have to try one of the white ones." She smiled slyly as she handed one to him.

"White one?" Kyle asked as he took the light-husked fruit from Poe and began the process of opening it. "So do you know this Nigel? He's actually the reason we walked all the way out here."

"Nigel? Yea I know him. He's…uh…different. You'll see." Poe said as she sat on the bed next to Kyle.

Pulling out pieces of the white fruit, Kyle's face was twisted into a look of disgust as it dripped thick, white juice. "Looks gross." He added as he dropped a small piece into his mouth. Poe just laughed at the reaction she thought he'd have. "Okay, it's not bad…different."

Kyle didn't talk as he ate, he found that he was much hungrier and thirstier than he even thought he was. Poe took the opportunity to tell him about waiting outside the beach house for him, following Tom up the side of the hill, their fall from the hill, and their rescue by the pale "angels". She told him that Tom was

190

in some kind of coma next door, that he had hit his head when they fell from the hill. As she told her story Kyle kept shoving pieces of fruit into his mouth, his expression never changed so Poe finally asked, "Are you even listening to me?"

After waiting for his mouth to finish processing the juice and lumps of fruit, Kyle responded, "I'm listening. To tell you the truth, I knew you were here, that you were okay, and that Tom wasn't."

Poe stared disbelieving at Kyle as he finished his final chunks of fruit, wiped his mouth with the back of his hand, and tossed the empty husk onto the floor next to the husks of the first two he had eaten. He then decided to tell her about what had happened at the beach house and the changes he'd felt since.

After an annotated version of his brush with the worms, Poe unable to comment, her face frozen in a look of disbelief, he started to tell her about meeting Darla and Otto but she stopped him because, while he was out, she had met them herself. Otto and Darla told her all about finding Kyle covered in blood next to the beach house and their long walk across the dry sea.

"So you have some kind of mental... connection with this...this world?" Poe asked as she ran her hands through her long hair and thought about what Kyle had told her.

"I guess," Kyle answered. "I still don't know how to use it very well, most of what I see is nonsense. I think it's getting stronger, though." He closed his eyes and thought for a moment. "We have to get out of here, leave this world."

Poe stared at Kyle hoping that he was going to continue with some idea or plan that he had come up with. When he didn't she placed her hand on his shoulder and asked the obvious question, "How?"

Kyle locked eyes with Poe then looked around their small chamber as if the answer was near them somewhere. He finally answered, "I don't know. Andy brought us here, maybe he can bring us back. It's the only idea I have."

"His name is Andy?" Poe asked.

Kyle didn't answer right away and when he finally did he decided to tell her, "He says he's my brother but I don't really want to believe him." After another pause, he added, "I really think he is, though."

With a look of shock on her pretty face, Poe just stared as she tried to decide what this new information meant to her.

"I'm sorry. I still need to find my parents. I want to know if it's true." Kyle said sadly. "My parents are here, in this world somewhere. Once I find them I am going to find Andy and make him take me home…and you too."

Deciding the conversation was more than she wanted to think about at the moment, Poe changed the subject. "Well, for now, we can just focus on getting you back on your feet. Maybe Nigel knows something about your parents or a way we can get home."

Surprising Poe, Kyle turned to her and wrapped his arms around her again. "I hope you're right. Either way, I will get us back home." He reassured her and she leaned in and kissed his cheek.

With his heart beating so hard and fast that it was nearly audible in the silence of the room, Kyle lifted his head and looked into Poe's beautiful face. His mouth was suddenly much too dry as he thought about how beautiful she really was. Gathering as much courage as he could, he ran his hand along the side of her soft cheek and into her long, dark hair. Almost without thought, he leaned in and touched his lips to hers. With eyes wide open they kissed. Slow and gentle at first, things were happening so suddenly. Her lips were soft and felt amazing. With his hand now deep in her hair, on the back of her head and her hands on his flush cheeks their kiss became much more passionate. His whole body tingled as if electricity was coursing through his veins along with his blood. He sensed her eagerness so, as gently as he could, he guided her, still locked at the lips, onto her back on the moss bed. His excitement now apparent he placed his free, right hand under her shirt and onto her bare stomach. Her skin was soft and warm as his hand crept slowly up, fingertips barely touching the skin. Goosebumps raised on her skin as he slowly pushed his hand under her bra to the small swell of her breast. Their moment of pleasure seemed almost surreal against the backdrop of the drab, sad world around them. The very stone that surrounded them seemed to join in their ecstasy, the rocks glowing in the wall seemed slightly brighter and the moss on their bed visibly began growing.

Fifteen

"Worms?" Nigel said coolly though a slight hint of concern had entered his usual, almost monotone voice. "I have not seen any here."

Otto, Darla, and Nigel were all seated in the corner of the cone's large cavern. Darla had a look of genuine concern on her face as she talked with Nigel. Otto was turned so that he could watch the inhabitants of the Cone, something he had enjoyed since his first time visiting.

"These "worms" you are asking about were once an incredibly powerful part of this place. A single, ancient being irrevocably tied to our world. What you might call a god." Nigel began. "Weakened but still powerful it decays along with everything else. The influence from the building you have escaped from has spread for a very long time. It cannot be stopped anymore. Once those worms are gone everything else will follow."

"So these worms.... went.... crazy? You don't think they'd be here?" Darla asked as the thought of what happened to Kyle flashed within her memory.

Standing from his seat Nigel looked to Darla and answered, "I would not say they went "crazy". It's more like a trapped, injured animal clawing for life. I believe we are safe here. Please do not worry, Darla." Saying no more, he suddenly walked away.

"I'd like to see 'em swim with those weird wings of theirs," Otto said as if he had completely missed the conversation that had just taken place behind him.

***

With Poe and Kyle standing hand-in-hand at the entrance to Tom's chamber, he lied as still as a dead man, unaware of their presence. The small, slow movements of his chest the only clue to the faint fire of life still burning within him and the gash on the side of his head was nearly healed.

"Poor Tom. I really hope he comes out of it." Kyle said sadly though he really didn't think Tom would ever wake up, he had been asleep for too long. He had also hoped that this was what all the fear he had been feeling was about but, deep down, he knew this wasn't it. There was something else and he could still feel it, even after making love to Poe, even with her small, delicate hand holding his, even with her beautiful, smiling eyes looking into his own, he felt something terrible. The fear and anxiousness made his stomach hurt and he hated it, he wanted to find the fastest way out of this place.

Kyle kissed Poe's cheek as they turned to leave Tom's room. This was suddenly one of his favorite things to do and he wished everything was fine and he could just kiss this beautiful girl for days, but things were far from fine. Still hand in hand, the pair made their way down the hall and into the large, main cavern.

A couple things suddenly made sense to Kyle as he entered the huge, open, center cavern of the cone. He had seen the remains of some of these pale creatures in front of him in the room where he had first met Andy, where they prepared meals for The Mouth. He thought that they must also be the dreamy "ghosts" he had seen just before losing consciousness. A little montage of a flashback played in his mind of that butchering room and the beach house as he walked.

"That's Nigel," Poe said, pointing toward one of the pale creatures walking toward them.

As the creature came closer Kyle was able to see more of Nigel's human-like features and something within him found Nigel grotesque.

"Hello, Kyle. Happy to see you are well." Nigel stated plainly as he stopped in front of Poe and Kyle.

After a brief, involuntary pause to further study Nigel's strange features, Kyle returned Nigel's greeting, "Thanks. Nice place you have here."

Before anyone could say anything more, Nigel turned and began walking back into the cavern. With a motion of his hand, he told Poe and Kyle to follow and Kyle couldn't help but notice the strange, fleshy, folded wings on his back. He led them through the center of the cavern and to where the collection of carved tables and chairs were.

Once all three had found a seat at an empty table, Nigel started, "I know that you have questions for me. I will do my best to answer what I can."

"I appreciate that," Kyle said and he found that he suddenly had many more questions for this strange creature than he originally had. "Darla thinks that you may have some connection with this world. If that's true, I'm looking for my parents. I'm sure they are here somewhere."

Without pause or thought, Nigel answered, "I am surprised that you still question a connection to this world when you now share this connection. As for your parents.... I am afraid that I can offer no answers. I sense that many people are brought to this world. I am actually proof of that. To tell you where two have gone would be nearly impossible."

For a few moments, Kyle was unable to get his tongue to work. Hearing Nigel mention what he had been feeling, shocked him slightly and not hearing an answer about his parents disappointed him. With the subject of his parent's whereabouts already moot, he decided that all the questions he had about Nigel's history, the specifics of his new power, and this strange new world were no longer important so he asked the other big question he had, "Is there a way for us to leave this place?"

This time, Nigel actually appeared to take a few moments to think about Kyle's question before he finally offered, "I cannot say for sure but if there is a way back to your own world it will be back through the door that led you here. Put your skin on the rock and you will find that this world is decaying…dying. Even if we could destroy the one that brought you here, as we have tried many times, the cut is too deep now and soon nothing we are discussing will matter."

"Well, that's morbid," Poe said with a muted look of horror on her face.

Nigel continued, "It is true. The creature that shared its power with you, Kyle, was once a powerful and essential part of this world. For a long time, it has been corrupted by the powerful beast that consumes our kind.... well your kind also… everything really."

"The worms?" Kyle asked.

"Yes. My father did tell me they strongly resembled what are worms in your world." Nigel answered and then looked out into the large cavern. Once he turned back to Kyle and Poe he said, "I am sure you have felt it. There is something terrible coming and I think that I may know what that terrible thing may be. We must remain alert until our waters return. Kyle, you are welcome to stay here with us as I now see there is a connection between you and Poe. Though I cannot say that you will be any safer here."

After shooting Poe a sweet smile, Kyle answered, "Thank you but I want to continue looking for my parents and then I want to find a way back home." He would have asked Nigel what he thought the terrible thing coming was but he didn't really think he'd get much of an answer, there seemed to be something that he didn't want to tell them.

"I understand. You will need to head back soon. You do not want to be caught in the sea when it returns. I will let Otto and Darla know of your decision." Nigel said as he stood from his seat, he then turned and walked away.

"He does that a lot," Poe said with a small laugh. "So where are we going to look for your parents?" She asked as she ran her delicate fingers tracing along the veins on the top of Kyle's hand.

Staring at the rough tabletop, Kyle thought for a while then answered, "I honestly don't know. Maybe, if I practice a little more, I can use this connection thing to find some answers. I still have that severed hand back in Darla and Otto's cave so we might be able to go back to our little dome. We'll leave Tom here, he'll be taken care of and there's no way we can carry him all the way back."

Thinking to himself that now was as good a time as any to try his power again, Kyle rose from the table and walked the short distance to the rough, stone wall. With Poe watching curiously from behind him he placed both his palms to the wall. Instantly, his brain became a sickening show of flashing images and his belly full of fruit churned as he was consumed by a myriad of feelings. The strongest feeling was fear, the type of fear you'd feel if you walked around a dark corner and met some monster face to face. With sweat already beading on his forehead and upper lip, he fought as hard as his brain could in an attempt to control the deluge of information. Slowly, with an incredible amount of concentration, he was able to make sense of some of the information he was getting. He could actually feel the sickness of the world he was touching, could feel it weakening. He saw a visage, hazy as if through frosted glass, of what could only be The Mouth and he sensed that this awful creature was angry. In all he saw and felt though he couldn't sense his parents or even Andy and he still couldn't see what terrible thing seemed to be so close that it might be standing directly behind him.

Now drenched in sweat, Kyle dropped his hands from the wall and just stood for a moment as his mind and heart settled. Once deciding he felt well enough to turn around, he turned and met eyes with Poe who was staring at him with a look of concern and wonder on her pretty face.

Rushing to Kyle's side, Poe threw her arms loosely around him and asked, "Are you okay? What did you see?"

As Kyle took a few steps toward the table he answered, "Nothing really. We should leave here as soon as we can. There is something…dammit, I couldn't see it…something awful. Near."

Placing a reassuring hand on Kyle's shoulder, Poe said, "Okay. Let's find your friends and see when we can leave."

Kyle and Poe found Otto and Darla conversing with Nigel near the tapering column at the center of the cavern that contained the staircase. As they approached, Kyle noticed that the conversation in front of them ended abruptly and they had all turned, looking at something. In fact, almost everyone had stopped and was now staring at something on the far end of the cavern. Turning toward the source of everyone's gaze, Kyle and

Poe stopped and stared, disbelieving. Near the opening in the far wall that led to the chambers wherein, Kyle had just recently awoken was Tom. He was on his feet and walking slowly toward them.

Poe cried happily, "Tom!" and started walking to meet him.

Feeling chill fingers run uncomfortably down his spine, Kyle ran after her. As he passed her he put his arm out as a way to tell her to "hold on" and he continued toward Tom. The closer he got to Tom the more his skin began to crawl with fear.

Tom was walking slowly but his eyes were wild with confusion and fear, the whites had turned blood red. Kyle stopped approaching, he had gotten close enough to notice how "round" the man looked. When he had seen Tom lying in his coma his mind took note of how thin he had become from his time unconscious, but now he looked much fuller; almost fat. His panicked, red eyes met Kyle's and Kyle noticed with horror that, not only was he rounder looking, his skin seemed to be moving just slightly. Unable to remove his eyes from what had been Tom, Kyle didn't notice that Darla, realizing something was really wrong, had run up just behind him with Otto fearfully following her.

"Tom?" Kyle asked apprehensively, his voice wavering with fear.

As Tom opened his mouth as if to answer, vomit poured like a waterfall from his gaping mouth. Looking closer though Kyle noticed that what was pouring from Tom's mouth was not vomit but a thick, unending stream of worms. Kyle stared in horror as cries from behind him echoed in the room. The worms pooled at Tom's feet, a swirling, undulating, grey mass that grew larger as he seemed to wither and deflate. Once the stream finally stopped and he resembled a week-old corpse, he looked one last time at Kyle who was still frozen in fear, his eyes rolled to the back of his head, and he fell to the floor dead.

There was little sound in the, now still, room except for Poe's quiet weeping and the gentle rush sound from the large mass of worms in front of Kyle. All the occupants of the cone that hadn't already fled were now staring toward that ever-changing blob of wriggling little worms as it crept across the floor toward Kyle. Once they were close enough, Kyle reacted with little thought and swatted at the worms as if to scatter them. What his open hand met was much firmer than he had anticipated and his swing was stopped halfway into the squirming mass. His hand and most of his forearm were quickly engulfed by the little worms and the horrible show that started in his brain stopped him cold. Frozen, with his right arm, suspended within the body of worms, his mind was, once again, linked with the collective conscious of the ancient worms. Images flooded his mind again, most were meaningless but he was able to understand that this creature was sick and actually quite weak. Like someone in a lucid dream, he wrestled for as much control of his mind as he could and, instead of just being "probed" by the worms, he reached within the mind of the worms. The experience began as incredibly surreal and he almost felt as if he were physically outside his own body, for the moment he couldn't feel the creepy sensation of the worms on his skin. He could sense past things that didn't belong to him, he could feel a sense of the worm's departure from part of its world to an out of control, dying mess, he could feel The Mouth's touch on them like the stink of disease. Rummaging through the worm's collective conscious like someone rifling through the scattered pages of a journal, he found something familiar. It was his parents. He could see them now, feel their presence as if they were standing close enough to touch. He wanted to call out to them but he didn't know how to talk within this place. If they were alive or not he couldn't sense and, if alive, he couldn't figure out exactly where they were. The possibility that they were now an actual part of the worms whispered briefly within his scattered thoughts. They were only ghosts, half-remembered faces in the subconscious of this world's old god.

Kyle was suddenly aware of something familiar but he couldn't think straight while floating within the confusion of the worm's mind, which had suddenly become much more active, so he began to let go. All at once he knew what he sensed, it was fire. He could feel the worms on his skin again, they were now caressing almost half his body. He could also smell something disgusting, something burning. The large cavern room was beginning to come back into focus around him, the worms were losing their grip on his mind. Before he had fully made the transition from the mental to the physical, he suddenly felt himself being pulled backward violently.

Chaos was what Kyle came back to, like someone waking from a deep sleep. Now aware that he was sitting on the ground with two large arms under his armpits that had to be Otto's, Kyle desperately tried to shake the confusion and haze from his mind. Once his eyes would focus again he saw what had unfolded while he was gone. Darla had her flask in one hand and a gold lighter open and lit in her other hand. Periodically she was spitting bright fireballs at the scattering worms, the floor was littered with many small, charred flecks. As Otto continued to drag Kyle across the rough floor away from the remaining, dispersed worms, Kyle noticed that the room had cleared out and only he, Otto, and Darla were left.

"I'm up now, Otto," Kyle said, his ass beginning to hurt from being drug over the stone floor. A sudden and strong sense of pity hit him as he composed himself, it was for the worms.

That what he once saw as frightening and possibly even evil he now felt sorry for. Their grip was loosening.

Having dragged Kyle to almost the complete opposite side of the room from Darla, Otto stopped and helped Kyle up. "Sorry man. That was just freaky. Wanted to get you outta there."

Watching Darla finish up the last of the liquid in her flask with a couple final, small fireballs aimed at a few retreating worms, Kyle sadly said, "They weren't trying to hurt me."

"She didn't even hesitate, she thought they were going to kill you. Lucky she had that lighter on her, but really I don't think she's ever without her lighter and that flask of shit." Otto said seriously.

Thinking he was feeling some residual "creepy-crawlies" from having the worms on him again, Kyle looked down at his right arm and found a couple worms still clinging to some arm hairs. With a dismissive brush, he sent all but one to the floor. The final one he picked up between his thumb and forefinger. For a moment he let it wriggle hopelessly between his fingers before he set it softly on the ground and watched it retreat. Sadness gripped him then as he thought of his parents and of this sad, decaying world. He knew now that finding his parents and escaping from this place were paramount, with death the only other alternative.

"Godammit, Kyle, you need to stop doing shit like that!" Darla said as she approached Kyle and Otto. Her voice boomed in the cavern. "Did you see any of that? That was badass! Those little fuckers went running!"

"I saw a little. Thank you but they weren't trying to harm me." Kyle answered sincerely. "I think they were trying to even save Tom, or at least save us *from* him."

Darla gave Kyle a little nod to say 'You're welcome.' but his words echoed in her mind and she wondered if her reaction had been right. Even though she wasn't as intimate with this world as Kyle apparently was she had known for a long time that things here were not going well.

Slowly the inhabitants of the cone began to filter back into the room. One of the first was Poe and she ran up and embraced Kyle, her eyes swollen and red. "I want to leave this place." She whispered to Kyle and he responded with a nod of his head.

"Me too... Me too."

"You have only caused further injury to an already weakened creature." The deep and loud voice of Nigel proclaimed as he walked up to them. His tone bordered on angry but was tamed by his own feeling of futility. "It would be my guess that they were stopping your friend from enacting something terrible. He had been corrupted by the same creature that has been consuming this world without constraint. It does not matter, though, the ties that bind our world together are decaying quickly.

"We need to get out of here," Darla said with a sound of urgency. "The waters will be returning soon."

With his arm firmly around Poe's shoulders, Kyle said, "I'm sick of running and I'm sick of this place. No offense, Nigel. It's time to meet this "Mouth" guy."

"Do as you will. I am unsure that there is anything that can be done at this point." Nigel said solemnly. "Prepare yourselves for departure and I will allow you out."

Before they would leave the cone they quickly prepared a funeral pyre for Tom in the large pool. He was laid on a hastily constructed mass of dried moss that the pale ones furnished. Darla and her trusty lighter provided the flame. The stone fortress was silent as the large room, filled nearly to capacity, was engulfed in the orange glow of fire. For a while, had anyone seen the cone, they would have thought that it resembled a small volcano as Tom's decimated body fed the fire. Nigel, Poe, Otto, and Darla were all that occupied the room by the time the blaze had reduced to only a few small, smoldering islands of ashes floating on the dirty surface of the pool.

"Goodbye, Tom," Poe said, breaking the silence of the large room.

Following her lead, Kyle added, "Yea.... bye, Tom. I didn't know you.... very well but.... you didn't deserve this. See ya."

Nigel gave each of them a look and a quick nod that they all understood. Reluctantly, they all followed Nigel into the water of the pool and disappeared beneath its surface.

The water they swam in was incredibly warm from sitting stagnant, embraced by the warm stone and each of them experienced varying degrees of mental and physical effects during their brief swim, Kyle had to really concentrate to keep from succumbing to it. Following Nigel toward the bottom of the pool, they swam back up into a water-filled passageway that curved upwards like the trap on a toilet. At the top of the curve, they resurfaced and climbed from the water into a small tunnel. They followed Nigel down the other side of the curved passage to where it ended at a smooth wall of stone. The group stood watching Nigel, dripping and silent as he approached the smooth wall and placed both his hands upon the stone. After a moment the wall began to shift and move to the side, revealing first just a sliver of the dead, maroon sky. Standing there watching the wall open for them, Poe thought to herself that the sky looked to be an even darker shade of maroon than she remembered.

With the wall open enough for the group to fit through, they all said a quick and solemn goodbye to Nigel and made their way outside. Kyle was relieved to find the descent much easier and faster than the last time he had been on the side of the cone. Once the four had slid and jumped to the base of the rock they all noiselessly begin to follow Darla across the flat expanse of seabed before them.

Sensing Darla's urgency and the thought of the ground they were walking on covered with water, their pace was quick. No one spoke and they walked almost single file with Otto pulling up the rear. Poe walked briskly behind Kyle, holding his hand for periods as long as they could each take. No one really knew how long they had been walking when they all noticed the ground becoming much softer and wetter. Keeping their pace no one said a thing.

Kyle's mind was heavy as he walked and he only left the thought of his parents to come up with ideas to kill The Mouth and Andy. He had few, if any, good ideas and didn't really know how he'd get himself and Poe back to their home. All he really knew for sure was that The Mouth and Andy would die at his hand. The anger that had started as just a small fire within him when he had first arrived in the barn was now a blaze that consumed him and only grew brighter the more he thought about it. As his feet began to slosh in what had now become muck he tried to wipe his tears without Poe noticing, but he failed.

Poe was beginning to understand that she loved Kyle but she really held no hope for anything more than dying at the hands of one of the long-armed monsters from the barn. She knew that Kyle would be returning to that large building and she knew that he had revenge on his mind. As she walked she thought back on her short life and wondered how and when death would finally catch up to her. She also wondered if the ground seemed to be getting much wetter.

Tired and solemn, the group took a short break to catch their breath and eat a fruit though none of them felt much like eating. Leaning against a large stone, Kyle noticed that the ground they were standing on was now covered in a small layer of water. He had always envisioned the sea returning in a tsunami-like wave but he now thought that it must return from the ground. For the first time since leaving the cone, he felt something other than anger and sadness, he feared the returning water. He knew from his walk to the cone that they still must have a sizeable distance yet to cover.

After only a short respite, Darla got everyone back onto their feet and walking again. Each step they took now caused a splash and neither could deny that their time was limited. Even Otto was keeping up with everyone's' quickening pace, his breaths coming in great, audible heaves.

In what felt like an incredibly short amount of time, the water had reached their knees. They were all splashing through the water in a panicked, clumsy run. The shore was still not within sight and each moment that passed meant their steps became more labored. Each of them, especially Otto, was on the verge of paralyzing exhaustion and hope of survival melted away to reveal thoughts of final moments, treading water beneath a dark, maroon sky.

Darla, being the shortest, was the first that had to switch to a kind of mixture of running and swimming. By the time Kyle and Poe were to the point where their feet would lose traction because they were beginning to float, Darla had switched to swimming and the group's collective momentum had slowed to a crawl.

"I...I can't go any farther," Darla said as she stopped and began treading water.

The only one still able to stand on solid ground but almost overcome with exhaustion, Otto replied, "But I can't see the shore yet Darla! Oh fuck... fuck we're gonna die out here!"

Otto may have wanted Darla to argue with him and offer some way of getting them safely to shore but she didn't, she only bobbed silently in the water.

As the water slowly rose, the group tried swimming but would only cover a short distance before they would have to stop and tread water. Finding himself in a strange calm, Kyle noticed that the small, spider-like creatures he had seen on the ground were now swimming around them in incredible numbers; their little "legs" tickled any exposed skin. He couldn't help but think that watching them spiral through the water could have been beautiful under different circumstances.

The water was nearly at its full depth when the group silently decided to give up. Each tread water and waited for the moment their muscles would fatigue and they'd dip below the surface. Their final breath would be of water.

With an incredible amount of concentration, Kyle was successfully staving off the strong force on his mind from being in contact with the water around him. He was getting pretty good at it. Slowly he paddled himself through the water up to Poe, he wanted to kiss her. Without saying a word, Poe looked as if she had been thinking the same thing, he pressed his lips tightly against hers. With his lips still locked with Poe's, Kyle felt a sudden and unmistakable feeling of hope and comfort envelope him. He couldn't identify it at first, he figured it had to be the kiss, but, with some concentration, he knew that Nigel and some of his family were on their way, flying through the water on their pale, fleshy wings. An image floated through his brain of swift, strange angels.

"We're going to be okay." Kyle suddenly said, his voice alarming after the group's time in silence.

No one answered Kyle despite the sincerity in what he said. Neither of them felt what he did and their tired minds were void of hope.

Noticing that none of them were taking what he said seriously, Kyle added, "Nigel is coming, he'll be here soon." He couldn't help but let a relieved smile bend his lips.

Reluctantly, everyone's haggard expressions softened with the tiniest glimmer of hope as they bobbed in the rising water. None, except Kyle, would be fully convinced until they saw the pronounced ripple coming toward them and soon they saw just that. Within the swell, that bowed the top of the still water was a group of pale ones flying in the water like large birds. They were quickly moving toward them.

Sixteen

Exhausted but safe back on the shore, Kyle, Otto, Darla, and Poe said their thanks to a group of six cone dwellers that included Nigel. The radical change in state of mind from the belief in imminent death to being brought to safety had a profound effect on all of them. Even so, they all decided to head back to Otto and Darla's cave to rest up and try to come up with a plan of attack. The cone dwellers agreed to stay close to the shore and help once the group decided to head up the hill toward the large building.

"The air is colder now, isn't it? And the sky seems darker." Otto mentioned as the foursome began their climb up to the entrance of the cave.

Otto was the first to mention it but he was definitely not the first to think it. They had all noticed the drop in temperature and the darkening sky but it seemed to be human nature to try and dismiss something that brings you more fear. There was no denying it, though, they didn't need Kyle's connection to feel the world around them slowly dying.

"It is," Kyle answered plainly. He really didn't feel much like talking, none of them really did. The journey back from the cone had taken a toll on all of them, Darla especially.

No one spoke again, even at the small entrance to the cave they all just filed inside. Poe was the last one in and just followed Kyle's lead. The inside of the small cavern was cool, damp, and dark, the smell of smoke hung in the thick air. After much coaxing, Darla was finally able to restart the remains of her last fire. Still wet and cold, she decided to make a larger one than she usually did and piled most of what she had onto the tiny fire. Once the moisture hissed out of her pile of dried fruit bush the flames blazed bright and warm. Still, without any words everyone found a place near the fire, Kyle happily held Poe who was quickly falling asleep.

***

Otto was the first up. He knew that he must have slept for quite some time because Darla's fire was out and the remaining ash wasn't even smoldering anymore. The cave was once again cool (almost cold) and completely dark except for a small amount of weak light coming from the open crags in the cave's roof. He crawled outside to leave everyone to sleep. He had always kind of enjoyed standing just outside the cave on the side of the hill looking out over the mirror-calm sea but now it felt different. The air had taken on a chill and the dark maroon sky was churning like some angry ocean. There was also a wind that tousled his messy, blond hair; he hadn't felt wind since the day before he woke up here. Goosebumps stood up on his skin and he hated the feeling within him that something terrible was happening all around him.

After standing there for what felt like hours to Otto, Kyle and Poe squeezed out of the cave. They were still trying to rub the remaining sleep from their eyes and they both looked chilled.

Poe collected her thoughts, looked at Kyle worriedly, and said, "It's gotten worse. It's almost cold out now. God look at the sky...and it's windy!"

With an eerie calm to his voice, Kyle assured Poe, "We have time. What you're seeing is just more symptoms of a disease that has been killing this world for a long time. It's that disease that I'm going to find once Darla wakes up."

"We're all going. I want to see this piece of shit." Otto said as he looked toward the direction of the large building.

Following Otto's gaze, Kyle responded, "I'm not going to argue, in fact, I'm sure I'll need the help just to get close to him. We did kill two of those long-armed freaks though when we escaped."

"Really? Well, I'm sure we'll all have the opportunity to kill some more of those soon." Otto laughed, placing a strong hand on Kyle's back.

"I'm coming with too," Poe added as she tried to get as close to Kyle as she could for his warmth.

Drawing Poe into his chest, Kyle responded, "Like I said, I'm not going to argue. Just please be careful. I still plan on getting us out of here."

As Kyle held Poe close and they all stared out at the calm sea a voice from behind them made them jump, "Who's ready to storm that ugly castle on the hill?"

Laughing, everyone turned around to Darla who was emerging from the cave. She stood next to the rest and said, "We must have slept forever.... I see things have gotten nicer out here. I don't know about all of you but I'm feeling pretty good." After staring out over the decaying world for a few moments she continued, "I say we get something to eat then we might be able to come up with some weapons."

"Weapons?" Kyle asked intrigued. After Darla had supplied him with shoes he wouldn't doubt she had some weapons in her little pile.

Turning back toward the cave, Darla replied, "We'll see what I've got."

In preparation, they each ate as much fruit as they thought they needed. Using a small, dim flashlight, Darla found a mismatched pair of sandals for Poe that were much too big but after a few strips ripped from an old t-shirt they stayed on. As for weapons, all that Darla was able to scrounge up were two box cutters, a well used four-inch folding knife, and the Leatherman that she usually carried herself. Kyle and Poe each took one of the box cutters and Otto took the folding knife. It wasn't much but each felt a small amount of power from the blade they held and each silently fantasized about using their meager weapons on the monsters they would soon encounter.

"So what's the plan?" Otto asked.

Kyle and Darla exchanged glances that conveyed that neither really had an answer. Thinking for a moment, Darla responded, "I think the main room of that place is under those towers. I've been back in that building but only next to the barn area and into that killing room. We really don't have much to go on. I just say we try and find that main room and do all we can to kill this thing."

"Sounds good to me I guess. S'pose there really isn't any more planning we could do," Otto said.

"This is it. We're going to kill the motherfucker that brought us to this shithole." Kyle said with the excitement of a soldier before battle. His severed hand was tucked in its place in his waistband and he had tethered his box cutter to his right wrist with some string he had found.

"Oh, Kyle, I have one more surprise for you before we do this," Darla said as she headed back to her pile of stuff. After a little digging, she returned to the group and held up what she had found.

"I have one," Kyle said as Darla held up a severed, three-fingered hand.

"Not like this one you don't," Darla said and she pushed the hand closer to Kyle.

Kyle's eyes widened as he realized what Darla must be holding. "That's a left hand isn't it?"

Darla nodded and said, "Have you seen those creepy, fat monsters down there? Usually, when the long-armed monsters kill the fat ones they destroy all the left hands but take the rights."

"Oh, yea! We watched them build." Poe said excitedly.

Realizing the power of two builder hands, Kyle took the hand and secured it in his waistband opposite the first one he procured.

Feeling as ready as any of them would, they all squeezed out of the cave and started down the hill. The mood and collective feeling of the group were vastly different than it was when they were headed in the opposite direction, wet, fatigued, and hopeless. Now they felt as if pure adrenaline were pumping through their veins. Any fear they had was eclipsed by their energy and excitement and they walked with a stride that spoke of their confidence.

Beneath an increasingly angry sky and bombarded by a cool breeze that had turned into a cold wind the group started across the long beach with the beach house on their right and the large building on the hill to their left. No one needed a cerebral connection to the world to feel that eyes were upon them and their presence wasn't a surprise. No one had to say a word for everyone's gaze to converge on the barren land between them and the large building on the hill. Quickly coming down the hill were four shapes, still tiny from the distance, unmistakably the long-armed butchers.

"Here we go, guys," Otto said as a little fear began to filter back in.

As they watched the four shapes quickly grow in size, Kyle got down on his knees and placed his palms to the dirt. Rested and, for the first time in a while, clear-headed he was able to control the incoming feelings and images. It also helped that the intensity of the information had lessened. After only a few moments he stood up and said disappointedly, "They know we're coming."

"I think I could have told you that, Miss Cleo," Darla said with the thick accent of sarcasm.

Weapons out and held at the ready, the four of them stood waiting for the fast moving butchers to initiate the first battle. When the creatures were only about 80 yards away the beasts faltered and turned to their left. No one had noticed the six pale creatures emerge from the water and cross the beach to engage the butchers. Kyle was the first to start running toward the fight. Everyone else followed as soon as they saw him move.

The cone-dwellers seemed to be holding their own avoiding the strong, deadly arms of the butchers and they looked to be defending themselves with small spikes that had unsheathed at the base of their palms. It was only a matter of time, though, the pale creatures were not warriors, their home was in the water and the butchers seemed to be born for killing. Just as Kyle arrived at the edge of the chaos one of the cone dwellers was tossed so high into the air that there would be no way it would survive once it landed, he averted his gaze just in time to see another cone-dweller being pulled into two equal sized pieces within a spraying cloud of dark, green blood. Strange, deep screams echoed loudly in his mind as he ran.

With his box cutter cocked in his right hand, ready as if
he were holding a broad sword, Kyle ran toward the nearest
butcher which was currently occupied trying to grab one of the
quick and slippery cone-dwellers. Sand kicking up from his
heels, his heart was pounding with the quick beat of a labored
engine, and his face was twisted with fury and determination as
he lunged toward the butcher. With a swing of his right arm in a
wide arc that would have looked right at home in any ninja film,
he sunk the razor of his box cutter into the side of the butcher and
cut a two-foot gash. The gash fell open like a mouth, vomiting
out a pile of organs that looked pretty much like any pile of
innards except for the jet-black blood. Kyle quickly brought his
arm back to swing again, the disemboweled butcher howled with
a sound like an air raid siren and turned its attention to him.
About to make another wide slice he noticed that the blade of his
box cutter had shattered and all that remained was a worthless,
jagged, small chunk of metal. With an audible curse, he tossed
the useless tool aside just in time to avoid the large, grabbing
hands of the butcher. As the butcher shifted to grab at him again,
it's tiny eyes as wide as they'd open, it suddenly jerked and fell
forward into the dirt. Kyle stood over the large, motionless corpse
for a second of disbelief before he noticed the cone-dweller that
had been stabbing the butcher's pile of organs into a paste. He
meant to show him some kind of thanks but the cone dweller
slipped quickly away before he even had a chance.

Turning from the one dead butcher, Kyle watched as the surviving three monsters flailed and grabbed at the running, jumping, slashing, stabbing bodies that surrounded them. To his right, Poe was slashing at the front of a butcher that also had two cone-dwellers stabbing its back as they clung to it. Kyle ran up as the butcher tried to decide whether to try and grab the poking on its back or the slashing at its front. With no weapon now Kyle simply decided to try and overwhelm the already occupied butcher by punching it in its side as hard as he possibly could. Black blood rained down on him from the beast's multitude of wounds and he watched Poe from the corner of his vision. With a look of frustration, she plunged the two-inch box cutter blade into the creature's belly with the intention of opening it up but the monster stepped backward and the blood-covered box cutter slipped from her hand. Time seemed to slow as she looked at Kyle with wide eyes, knowing that she was pretty much defenseless. In that almost-frozen moment of time, she looked as if she knew an attack was coming and her only hope was to survive it. With the swing of one of its long arms the wounded butcher smacked Poe hard and sent her flying like a discarded rag doll, the sandals she had recently bound to her feet went flying off, each in a different direction.

With a horrified scream, Kyle watched Poe soar slowly and silently through the air and land far from the fray. Landing hard onto the rocky sand of the beach, she was still and did not move or try to stand. Reacting mostly out of rage he circled to the front of the weakening butcher and grabbed the plastic handle of Poe's box cutter still stuck in the creature's belly and pulled down on it with as much strength as he was capable of. Once again he spilled a mess of butcher guts to the black-blood-soaked ground. By the time the large body of the butcher fell to the ground Kyle was halfway to Poe's body which was unmoving and still in the same position she had landed in. Kyle would have been almost unrecognizable to her as he knelt beside her, most of his features were covered by glistening, black blood and his hair was slicked back from his forehead. As carefully as he could be he turned Poe over and checked her out. To his relief, though she was unconscious, she was still breathing and seemed to be okay. With a gingerness that spoke to his love for her, he did his best to make sure she was lying comfortable and safe, as much as he could with nothing but rocks and loose dirt.

After placing a kiss on Poe's filthy forehead, Kyle stood and started to walk back toward the fight. The ground in front of him looked like a war zone, with blood, guts, and the bodies of butchers and cone dwellers soaking in the dirt. One of the remaining two butchers was swinging its great arms toward Otto and the other was fighting off the only two remaining cone dwellers, one of which was Nigel. Darla was propped up against a pile of large stones with a grimaced look of pain on her face, she appeared to have an injured arm. As Kyle approached he tried to formulate a plan of attack and he suddenly realized that in his rush to check on Poe he must have dropped her box cutter. Without anything that could be used as a weapon he paused and looked around him for a large stone (it worked once, it could work again) or anything he could use. Suddenly an idea jumped to the front of his thoughts. It was crazy and if it didn't work the first time he'd be in a spot where he'd be susceptible but it was the only idea he had and Otto and the cone dwellers were showing definite signs of fatigue. He had to act. Bending to the ground, he filled both his fists with as much loose dirt as his hands could carry and ran toward the butcher that Otto was trying to fight. For a brief moment, time seemed to slow to a crawl as he passed Otto and the cone dwellers, both of whom shot him a look of desperation. His concentration so intense in this moment that the only sound he heard was the quick, thunderous beats of his heart. Like a basketball player leaping for a game-winning dunk, he avoided the butcher's arms and jumped toward its small head and shoved his right fist into its mouth. All within mere moments he deposited his fistful of dirt into the back of the creature's mouth then traded his empty right hand for his left as he hung by the creatures shoulder. Once he shoved the second handful into the creature he dropped back to the ground. The butcher actually paused as it choked on the dirt that fell down its throat and filled its mouth. Chunks of wet dirt and saliva sprayed upward. Once it swallowed most of what Kyle fed it and the rest dropped from its mouth, Kyle grabbed the severed hand from the right side of his pants. Otto and the cave dwellers watched with curiosity and horror as Kyle placed the palm of the hand against the body of the butcher. As soon as the severed hand touched the creature's belly the butcher reacted with a violent jerk. Kyle continued to wave the hand back and forth, up and down, and in circles across the creature's body as it shook, blood and dirt spewed from its mouth. Kyle removed the severed hand and stepped aside as the creature fell over with a final vomit of blood.

"Motherfucker!" Otto screamed in celebration. "Jesus man that was awesome."

His chest heaving with each quick breath, Kyle turned to the final butcher just as it was distracted by the cone dwellers. His brain seemed almost to be drowning in adrenaline, fury and fighting were the only thoughts still occupying his head. Almost without thought he ran toward the hulking figure of the butcher, Otto followed, spurned by Kyle's intensity.

The last remaining butcher seemed fully aware of its odds and it began moving with the quick, intense movements of a cornered animal, desperate for survival. With a lightning-fast movement of one of its massive arms, it grabbed one of the cone dwellers stabbing at its back and flung it aside with almost no visual effort. With only Nigel left plunging his spikes madly into its flesh, it switched its attention to Kyle and Otto who were quickly approaching.

Still high on his past victories, Kyle flung himself at the butcher with another fist-full of dirt. He was intent on repeating his recent victory but the adrenaline filling his quickly beating heart gave him a false sense of confidence because, in reality, he was no warrior. He never was. Almost as soon as he landed on the great beast and clumsily tried to climb to its small head he was snatched by a massive hand. It felt like it would surely crush him as he was quickly lifted high in the air. His ribs ached from the pressure of the creature's fingers. Relief came all at once as he found himself airborne for only a few seconds, the rough ground came up quick and painfully ended his flight.

Otto used the slight distraction that Kyle caused the butcher to make his move, but he also was no warrior. He was big but he was definitely not a fighter. He knew the stakes though and, at this point, he wasn't even sure Kyle would survive this fight. With only a quick, thoughtless glance at Kyle landing hard in the rough sand he plowed head-first into the right leg of the butcher. It was like running into a tree except, unlike the tree, the leg gave a little in the loose sand. Grasping the leg like a football player desperately trying to make a tackle he strained and pushed a little more. It was just enough to push the butcher's leg just beyond its balancing point. Above him the creature faltered, a cone dweller still hacking and slashing at its back, and it finally fell forward. As the monster fell hard into the ground, Otto felt much the same burst of adrenaline that Kyle had been feeling and, without pause, he turned and lunged for its head. Acting purely on his most base survival instincts he fell upon the beast's tiny head and plunged his thick fingers into its eye sockets. With surprisingly little force, his fingers passed through its eyes, releasing a thick, warm fluid onto his hands. Without thought, he pressed his hands into its face with increasing pressure, ignoring the sickening sound of his fingers entering each successive layer. Once his large fingers were poking into its head as far as they could reach, nestled firmly in a thick, warm, wetness he clenched his hands and pulled the head violently toward him. Letting out an intense, adrenaline-fueled roar he didn't even notice that the large animal beneath him had stopped moving moments ago. Standing atop an unmoving mass the rage subsided, he removed his fingers from deep within the creature's skull. His face softened and he looked like someone that was just caught in the middle of a late night bout of sleepwalking. Looking at the gore covering his hands he looked a little sick and started walking toward where he saw Kyle land.

"Jesus dude...are you alright? That was a rough landing." Otto asked as he approached a bloody, worn looking man.

Kyle didn't respond. He was waiting for his heart and breath to catch up and he felt like collapsing. Death surrounded him and he knew that the job was far from done. The sight of Poe sitting up and staring directly at him brought him quickly back and he couldn't help but smile with relief, he even found himself giving her a little wave. He immediately started walking up to her and as he did he watched as Nigel, the only remaining cone dweller, grabbed as much of his brethren's remains as he could and started dragging them toward the water. Kyle thought to himself that the pale creatures probably wouldn't be returning.

"How do you feel?" Kyle asked Poe as he sat on the ground next to her.

With a little smile, she replied, "My head is killing me but I think I'm okay. I'll be sore tomorrow. You're disgusting by the way."

With only a smile Kyle brushed Poe's hair from her face and kissed her hard. With a last look into her gorgeous eyes, he rose from the dirt and walked toward where Otto was checking on Darla.

"Kyle?" Poe called after him but she knew what he was planning and she also knew nothing she said would stop him. If she thought that there was any chance of leaving that awful place she would have put up more of a fight but any hope she may have had was long gone. It made her incredibly sad to think of the life they could have had but she also knew that waking up in that human barn was the only way she would have met him. She did hope to see him again but without any hope, she saw that kiss as their goodbye. Tears fell from her eyes, leaving little trails of clean skin, as she watched him walk away.

"How's Darla?" Kyle asked as he walked up to Otto who was carefully helping her up.

"She broke her arm. It's not terrible but it's definitely broken. Let's head back to the cave, this is over." Otto replied as he started limping toward the direction of the cave.

"I'm still going up there," Kyle said.

Otto turned toward him with a look of anger. "What?! That's suicide! C'mon man, come back with us and we'll think of something else."

"I'm sorry but I'm going. I have to do this. If I die up there just know that I'm taking them with me."

"That sounds all heroic and everything but you saw what those long-armed freaks did to a group of us. There could be a hundred of 'em up there. Don't be stupid man!" Otto said even though he was beginning to realize that he was wasting his breath. "Let me go with you at least."

"Nah, you have to get Darla back to the cave... Poe can help you. This is my fight now and I'll do what I can." Kyle said and, without another word, he started walking toward the large building on the hill.

Otto just shook his head and started after Darla who had kept walking and was now helping a shaky Poe up from the ground. He knew he wouldn't see Kyle again and he kind of understood. There was little hope left in this place, he thought to himself. He looked up into the once dead and now angry sky, as he did he also wondered how long they'd have to hide in their little cave.

As Poe, Darla, and Otto slowly walked back to the cave, all of them limping from injuries, they didn't speak. They only listened to the sounds the new breeze made as it blew across the rocks and hills. They each immersed themselves in their own thoughts about hopelessness and death and the end of everything.

***

As Kyle walked and the building that once was his prison appeared larger he steeled himself and tried to push back his mounting fear. He expected to see more butchers emerge from somewhere around the building. He knew that by himself he wouldn't last long against another group of the creatures. He also really had no idea what he was going to do once he found Andy and The Mouth. A voice in the recess of his mind knew that if he made it inside he would end up dying within the walls of the big building on the hill. He just knew that he would do all he could to make sure Andy and The Mouth did exactly the same thing.

The reality of what Kyle was doing hit him hard as he got close to the high walls, there was also something else that unsettled him. His mind and body flashed in a similar way that they did when he touched the ground except the feeling was slight and felt dark. It made him feel dirty, well he was dirty (he tried wiping the black blood from his skin but found it greasy and it only smeared), but this was a dark feeling as if his insides were as dirty as his skin. He immediately hated this new feeling, it crawled through his mind much like the worms had. As he walked close enough to the building that he could have reached out and touched it he knew that he wanted this whole nightmare to be over as quickly as possible.

To his left, not far from where he was standing, was the part of the building he had thought of as "the barn", it made him think of Poe again. As he stared at the spot on the wall where he figured they had escaped from he couldn't help wonder how many people might still be in there. He knew that checking would take time that he really didn't think he had but he wouldn't feel right if he didn't. He was playing the part of the hero in this story, wasn't he? The thought of himself as a hero caused a tiny smile and he started toward the barn.

Once reaching the edge of the barn he decided to move a little farther down as he realized that if he had opened the wall where he was, he would have been standing right in the bathroom corner. Walking a safe distance from the corner of shit he paused hesitantly for a moment wondering what he'd find and not really wanting to ever see the inside of this building again. With a heavy sigh, he placed the severed palm against the wall. An opening gaped before him and as a familiar, sickening smell hit him, he apprehensively stepped through it. The inside of the building seemed even more horrible than last he was here. The stench of feces and rot was overwhelming.

"Is anyone in here?!" Kyle screamed, standing in the dim interior of the barn. No one answered.

It seemed strange he thought to himself if someone had opened the wall while he had been here he would have greeted them with jubilation. The room remained silent. Something within him told him to just turn and leave, continue with what you were doing before but he decided that he had to be sure that no one was still trapped here. Just like when he used to jog with Poe, he started a quick run along the wall of the large room, ghosts of memories made him feel uneasy as he did. His breathing quickened and his nose took in more of the awful stench. He ran a little faster so that he could complete his round and return to the outside again.

What he found in the corner where he had first met everyone caused him to stumble hard enough that he crashed to the dirt floor hard. Still lying on his belly in the dirt, patches of his shins and forearms beginning to bleed and stick with dirt, he stared at the rotting remains of four bodies. Picking himself up he couldn't take his eyes off the bodies, they were all at the same point of decay, their skin was black and almost seemed to be melting off of their bones. Each of the four was in a different position, two lying on their sides on the floor and the other two seated on hay bales, their mouths hung open, teeth bright against rotting flesh. Once on his feet, he felt like crying. He wasn't sure how or why they died but he knew of the fear and confusion they would have been feeling, here in this prison. When he finally tore his eyes from the horror he sprinted back toward the wall that he had entered. All he could think of was reaching the outside, the "fresh" air beyond the walls of the barn. He cursed himself for returning here. With the severed hand held outward, he slammed into the wall and just allowed himself to fall through it as it opened. Rolling onto his back, once outside, he stared into the angry, maroon sky and took huge gulps of air. A couple tears escaped the edges of his eyes as he did.

Not allowing himself too much time to recover, he rose, brushed himself off and started to walk along the wall again. As he walked he tried to center himself and prepare for his meeting, he wanted to make The Mouth pay for this nightmare it created.

He searched his mind for what Darla had said about the main part of the building being just beneath the two high towers. More and more he felt the world around him become dream-like. It was as if the line between the physical world and the world that existed within his mind was becoming less distinct. He also couldn't help but feel as if his subconscious was fighting back something. As he walked along the high walls of the building, sharp stabs of wind whipping around it, he could see flashes that seemed like old memories of the building being built; hundreds of the fat builders waving their hands and creating solid walls from loose dirt.

As Kyle followed the rounded edge of the wall that he had decided would probably lead him into the main chamber of the building and onto the battle that would probably claim his life he stopped suddenly. The severed hand he had been carrying in his hand dropped to the ground sending up a small puff of dust. Standing about ten feet in front of him were his parents. They stood, alive and well. His mother smiled and lovingly rested her head on his father's shoulder.

Everything felt wrong, like a really bad trip on some unknown drug. For what felt like the hundredth time in only the last few hours his stomach lurched and threatened to convulse.

Could what he felt from the worms have been wrong? He thought to himself as he stared at his smiling parents. They looked happy and healthy but something about them felt dangerous and wrong. The feeling that everything was a dream was never stronger as he thought about calling out to them but he felt that opening his mouth would mean vomiting to the point where the blood vessels beneath his eyes broke.

As both his mother and father opened their mouths as if to speak, Kyle felt as though he might lose consciousness again but he steeled himself to fight the awful feeling. With both their mouths opening and closing with the movements of people talking loudly his parents made sounds that were far from anything that could have been called "talking". Their mouths moved but the sounds that came out were frightening and alien and almost resembled the old sound of a dial-up modem. The grating noises they made became louder until he could almost feel them like invisible fingers. The anger and desire for revenge that had been burning so bright within him, driving him on toward his own death suddenly melted like light snow in a midday sun. He felt a strong urge to just lie on the dirt and let his parents (or whatever, whoever they were) take him but there was something- almost an imagined whisper, too quiet to really hear, trying to keep him from doing just that. The world around him spun and wavered as if he was a boxer about to succumb to one too many blows to the head.

Kyle was suddenly aware that he was on all fours, rough dirt cut uncomfortably into his palms. He was also aware that his mouth was acidic and sour and his lips wet. He had vomited again and he wasn't even sure how many times. This was it and he hadn't even made it into the building, hadn't even confronted The Mouth and Andy. No conviction left, he decided to just give in and close his eyes. The whisper egging him on was now a voice calling for him to rise and fight the sickness. With eyelids as heavy as anvils and his limbs shaking uncontrollably he looked up one last time to his parents. Their happy, smiling image faltered and suddenly became a grey, moving silhouette of two, indistinct people.

With the little consciousness he had left, Kyle thought to himself, 'Fuck... Fuck... Fuck... The Mouth.' A smoldering ember of anger within him brightened and sparked. He hated this world and especially the awful demon just beyond these walls. Seeing it create the silhouette of his happy parents fueled that ember of anger and it suddenly exploded into a blaze that coursed through him as if his blood were gasoline. The pace of his heart quickened and adrenaline mixed with his pumping blood to help clear his foggy mind. The world didn't clear up instantly but the desire to just lie down was long gone and he was fueled by a renewed feeling of power.

In that moment Kyle almost thought he could *hear* something deep in his mind give way like a locked door being forced open. He suddenly felt a power that went beyond a release of adrenaline, a power as ancient as the dirt beneath his fingers.

Within an instant everything was clear and the line between the physical and the mental was dissolved completely. Kyle understood that he was now part of this strange and alien world. He understood that his brother's connection, the gift from the worms, and even consuming the world's fruits helped to not just link him with the world but to make him a part of it in the same way a single tree is part of a large forest.

Feeling a new and wonderful feeling of peace and symbiosis, Kyle dug his fingers into the loose dirt. This world may be weak and dying but it was far from dead and he now had some of its power flowing through him. Like a thick fog being dissolved by the warmth of the sun his mind looked beyond the silhouette of his parents and, as if in response, they slowly dissolved like thick smoke in the stiff breeze.

Kyle stood up. He felt better than he had in a long, long time. Awake in a way that he had never felt, ever. He felt as if the world had an added dimension, one he could never really see before, except this dimension went beyond "seeing". As he walked up to the wall, the dirt at his feet hovered slightly around his shoes like metal fragments around a magnet. His mind was calm but felt full with images and feelings that were like old, intimate memories. He knew that his new powers wouldn't insure his success at what he was about to do but he also knew that they wouldn't hurt and, in the least, they'd help him see Andy and The Mouth dead.

With a calm coolness, he rubbed the palm of his own right hand on the rough surface of the wall in front of him. As his fingers ran over the coarse material he could feel the power holding the dirt and stone together, he could bring the entire building down if he wanted but he didn't want to. Not yet.

Seventeen

With just a thought and his own hand, Kyle opened the wall in front of him. What was beyond was only darkness, a darkness so absolute that he almost felt that if he reached out he'd be able to feel it, touch it, interlace it between his fingers. Before his brain could talk him out of it with fear, he plunged into that darkness. As soon as the wall behind him closed the inky blackness was replaced with the unmistakably beautiful light of sunshine. Profound confusion gripped him as he took in his new and surprisingly familiar surroundings. He instantly recognized the living room of his parents' home. The sunlight that was now warming his skin was filtered through his mother's old, sheer curtains that flapped lazily in the sweet smelling breeze coming through the open windows. Everything looked exactly as it had…when he was six. Vivid memories took up every thought in his head, memories of summer vacations, playing in the yard, the summer-song of the frogs and crickets, the intoxicating smell after a thunderstorm. A smile crept across his face as he became sure of the fact that, somewhere outside, his mother was tending to her flower gardens and his father was probably working on the lawnmower with the local oldies station blaring from a small, tinny radio in the garage. Some part of him knew that this couldn't be real, that the horror that he had felt not that long ago was what was actually real. He could almost feel the memories of The Mouth and his dying world fading…no, disappearing.

Kyle took a deep drag of the sweet, summer air and closed his eyes. He walked up to one of the living room windows and let the sun bathe his smiling face. It seemed like forever since he had felt the sun but he couldn't quite remember why. Quickly fading memories of a maroon sky and monsters were now only vague remainders of an awful dream. He felt happier than he had in any recent memory.

"What should I do first?" Kyle thought to himself as he thought about grabbing his fishing pole or hopping on his bike. It was definitely going to be a good summer.

As Kyle started to push open the screen door that led out of the home's back door to the lush, green, inviting lawn, a loud noise from the room directly above the living room, his parents' bedroom, stopped him. 'Who could be up there?' he thought as he listened for any more sounds that may help answer his question. There was another sound, this one louder than the first and loud enough to make Kyle jump slightly. It sounded as if someone was dropping a hammer on the wood floor. After taking another glance beyond the screen door at the green wonderfulness of summer he decided he should check upstairs first. A large part of him protested and wanted only to run out that screen door and enjoy the long summer evening until his mother called into the warm night for him to get ready for bed. He had to find out what that sound was first, then he'd indulge in all the sun he possibly could.

Kyle slowly opened the old, wooden door to the home's second floor. Before him stretched the narrow, windowless stairway he had climbed countless times as a child. As he ascended the dark stairway, the noises above him continued and seemed to get louder each time they occurred. His joy now had a fear creeping over it like a bright, blue sky with a black thunderstorm overtaking it. A tiny whisper in the back of his mind told him that something was definitely wrong, he didn't know what but something wasn't right. As he reached the landing at the top of the stairs he turned briefly to his left. It was his old room. Even though the room was incredibly dark he could still just make out his model of the USS Enterprise hanging from the ceiling. Turning to his right, into his parents' room, fear iced his veins. The open windows were dark with night and there was only just enough light to make out the silhouette of a girl standing in the center of the empty room. His father's bookshelf was gone, there was no bed, no desk, it was all wrong. In the girl's right hand was a blunt object, obviously what she had been hitting the floor with.

The girl stared at him, she looked as if she had been trying to say something but there was no sound. Her lips moved but the empty room stayed deathly silent. Her beautiful black hair snaked around her head as if he were watching her from underwater. She must have realized that he couldn't hear her because her mouth now looked as if she were screaming something to him and yet still not a sound reached his ears.

Kyle felt dread and fear as the girl seemed to give up and walk toward him. Some small part within himself felt the girl seemed strangely familiar. With a look of sweetness that made Kyle take notice of how beautiful this girl was, she placed her hands on each of his cheeks and pulled him into a kiss. A voice so loud that it made his head instantly hurt boomed within his brain, "Snap out of it, Kyle!"

Kyle recoiled in horror and stared at the girl, her hair still floating around her. He opened his mouth to ask this strange girl how she got into his mind but no sound came from his lips, just as it hadn't for the girl. Before he could try again the girl pulled him violently into another kiss. "Please, Kyle. This isn't real! Remember! Come back to us! You'll die here."

A tiny spark of memory flashed across Kyle's mind and it filled him with fear and confusion. The memory was a name, Poe. He knew then that this girl kissing him, talking within his brain, was named Poe, short for Apollonia. He knew she was in trouble, he was too but he couldn't remember why. Thinking of the warm sunshine that he stood within not that long ago, he pushed Poe, pushed her as hard as he could. She fell backward, a look of shock and horror on her pretty face. When she landed on the wooden floor she splashed as if someone had dumped a bucket of water. She was gone and all that remained was a puddle soaking a wide patch in the old wood.

Kyle turned and ran as fast as he could down the stairs; he knew he had to find his parents. They would be outside, in the sun. They would tell him that everything was fine, they would tell him that the memories stirred up by Poe were nothing but a nightmare, but when he reached the living room, this time, the curtains were unmoving and the beautiful sunlight was replaced with only a bright, red glow.

This time, he didn't hesitate and threw open the screen door. The yard and the surrounding woods were just as he remembered, even the smell of green in the air. The sky was much different, though, it was clear but instead of a beautiful gradient of blue, it was blood red. Standing in the yard, he turned back toward the house, the peeling white paint was now a sick pink color, and he looked up into the window of the bedroom he just ran from. There was no sign there of the familiar girl he pushed. The ghost of her kiss was still on his lips.

Fear quickly began to replace the confusion in Kyle's mind. He was now sure that this place was wrong, even without the red sky, he knew this was definitely wrong. A part of him even screamed that this place wasn't real, that is was more like a dream. It was a dream that he had to wake from or he would die within his own mind. He just didn't know how to wake up, if that was even what he needed to do.

A sound like a nightmare freight train, a sound that could mean nothing good, made Kyle turn away from the house. The sound was coming from beyond the same field and woods where he saw that strange silhouette the night before he awoke in the barn. Something was coming, something big. He even thought he could see a shadow growing in the sky just over the trees beyond the field. Covered in the slimy sweat of fear, he watched as a form slowly appeared on the tree-covered horizon. The surreal feeling of being in a dream (no, a nightmare) became absolute as the approaching creature stepped beyond the forest and into the bare field. Consumed with fear he glanced once again at his childhood home and this time in the second story window that was, at one time, his parent's room there were two people slamming their fists into the glass. It was his parents, they looked scared and desperate as they beat at the window. They weren't hitting it to get his attention, they were hitting the glass to try and escape. They were trying to break the window, but they couldn't and they seemed to know it. The freight train like sound he had heard earlier had gotten loud enough to hurt his ears and he, once again, turned away from the house.

Its head was at least sixty feet from the ground. It walked on all fours and, in a very general sense, resembled a hairless dog; an incredibly deformed, hairless dog. Its long head ended in a grotesquely huge mouth with massive lips stretched around, what appeared to be, a mouthful of massive teeth. Its freakishly human-like eyes were pointed straight down at Kyle the entire time it slowly moved across the field. If the creature's alien face was capable of a recognizable expression, Kyle guessed it to be a desire to consume him.

Involuntarily, Kyle quietly mouthed the words, "The Mouth." He was sure that this saggy-skinned creature was named The Mouth and it was his business to eat people. Unsure of how he knew this, he was sure it was completely true and he felt as if a few more puzzle pieces came together in his scattered mind.

"I hope you believe me now." A calm, female voice said from behind Kyle accompanied by a hand on his shoulder. He didn't have to turn around to know that it was Poe.

Without turning to face Poe, Kyle responded, "It's coming back to me. Slowly. This is all a dream, isn't it? I mean, a nightmare."

"Something like that. You need to wake up or this is where you'll die."

The Mouth was moving slowly but it's long, thin legs covered a lot of ground with each step. There really was no way to outrun it. Kyle knew he'd have to figure out how to break the illusion before he and Poe disappeared into its cavernous maw.

He was sure now that this world existed only in his own brain, a dream designed by The Mouth using his own memories and thoughts. He guessed that he'd have to use those memories and thoughts to find wakefulness again. He needed to bring back all the memories that this dream had washed away. He turned around to face Poe. She was standing just behind him, her hair was now still and only flowed beautifully down onto her bare shoulders. The shock of seeing this beautiful, raven-haired girl standing nude, toes curled in the long grass, scattered his thoughts like a frightened school of fish. He figured the few moments it took for those thoughts to regroup was definitely worth it and, if anything, seeing her like this sparked a few more memories. The vague thought of a calm, silent sea and a cone of rock flittered just out of reach. He was suddenly possessed by that surreal feeling that comes with realizing you are in the grip of a dream.

As Kyle stared silently into Poe's eyes, the memories didn't exactly come rushing back but simply trickled randomly; butchers, severed hands, blood fruits, Andy. His brother, the thought made his skin crawl and that sensation on his skin brought back the memory that would save him and Poe from this dream world; worms. With that thought, Poe, whose beautiful face had been held in a look of hopeful anticipation, twisted into a look of absolute horror. He could feel what she was seeing. The sensation of his skin crawling had intensified into a feeling of something literally crawling beneath his skin. With little desire to see what Poe saw, he looked down at his arms. What he saw made his stomach convulse with a small dry heave. Every inch of skin that he could see was alive with movement. Movement that looked like a million agitated worms packed beneath his skin wriggling violently to find an escape. The second time his stomach convulsed it bent him in half and worms poured violently from his throat. Tears streamed down his cheeks as the deluge of worms continued to pour onto the grass. Poe stepped back in horror from the grey, wriggling pile that was forming in front of her.

When the waterfall finally ceased, leaving a huge, expanding pile of tiny worms, Kyle fell to his side and looked up at Poe, "I think I'll wake up now."

Eighteen

Poe gasped for breath as Otto dragged her out from the water and laid her on the beach. Her hunch had been correct and by immersing herself in the sea she had found a conduit through this world through the water. It wasn't as strong a connection as what Kyle had received from the worms and it took all her concentration but it had allowed her access to the world that The Mouth had created for Kyle. It allowed her to warn Kyle and hopefully wake him from the trap.

"You okay?" Otto asked as he stood over her. "What the hell did you just do??"

After a few more moments of easing her breathing, she answered, "I'm fine. I think he's going in there now. I don't.....something....like a voice but not a voice. It's weird, I just knew I had to help him. I think I did, though. Oh, my god, my head hurts." With the back of her hand, she brushed under her nose, smearing blood across her hand and face.

Darla, who had been sitting not far from where Otto had dragged Poe, said, "He's going to die up there. I don't know what just happened with you just now, in the water, but it doesn't matter."

Poe ignored Darla's comments and sat up. She didn't think she had ever felt as tired in her entire life as she did in this moment. Her head pounded with enough pain to make her a little nauseous. She really hoped Darla was wrong, she really wanted to see Kyle again. Still soaked, her breathing still heavy, Otto and Darla sitting silently behind her, she pulled her legs up to her chest and wondered what Kyle was doing up on the hill behind her.

***

It was Kyle's sense of smell that fired up first, just like when he awoke in the barn to the smell of shit and piss. This time, it definitely wasn't shit and piss, it was death. The stench of rotting flesh was so overwhelming he could actually taste it and his eyes began to water before he even opened them. Purposefully, he didn't open his eyes for a few moments. He was pretty sure he knew where he was and he wanted to collect himself a little before he faced it. The dream world that The Mouth had created for him was gone and he had arrived in this new place lying on his stomach. He was sure that most, if not all, of the scrambling that had occurred to his brain, was now gone and he felt ready to face that giant-mouthed, hairless dog he had seen in his dream. With a push, he simultaneously rose to his knees and opened his eyes. The room that he saw before him was more horrible than his imagination could have prepared him for and his mouth hung open in an involuntary, stupid expression.

The Mouth was staring at him from across a large, square room but the only part recognizable of the beast from his nightmare was its head. It was a little larger than a horse's and sat atop a lumpy, grayish mass that took up more than half the room.

Once he looked closer at the dog-like creature, Kyle saw The Mouth was not like he had been in the dream world; he had grown into an unmoving blob. The head was nestled in the main, large mass but even the walls and floor were covered with grey flesh. Fatty skin, with numerous, varying sizes of tumors protruding from it, the largest were split open and oozing, covered everything. Surrounding the huge pile that was now The Mouth were massive piles of discarded skin, bones, and body parts all in different stages of decay. Human arms stripped bare to the bone topped with hands black and rotting, leg bones with the meat of the feet rotting and dripping off, spots of the floor were covered with black puddles that were probably at one time human flesh. Even the high ceiling rained with the black liquid from rotting meat. Dim light from stones placed around the room illuminated the gore with a soft, sickly yellow glow.

It was seeing Andy standing close to The Mouth's left that finally broke his horror-induced trance. He looked toward the sick-looking man that was also his brother, unable to wipe the look of horror and disgust on his face. Andy looked calm and almost a little amused, this began to renew the anger-fire within Kyle. He felt his connection with this world, the power he drew from it just as strong as he had felt it whilst standing outside this room. All he had to do was turn around, touch the wall and he could bring The Mouth's entire "castle" down upon all of them.

"I wouldn't do that," Andy said, breaking the absolute silence in the large room.

Kyle stared into Andy's grey eyes with anger, "Why not... *brother*?"

"He is a part of this world now, a big part. Kill him and you kill this world and I know you don't want to do that.."

It suddenly occurred to Kyle. The Mouth was like cancer that had progressed too far, removing it would kill its host. Still locked in a staring contest with Andy, there was a change in Andy's gaze that Kyle took as a reluctant agreement to the sentiment. There had been a shift, though, a shift that he was sure that Andy and his boss could feel. Something changed, if even slightly when The Mouth had tried to trap him in his own brain. The worms weren't dead.

"This world needs a god. Don't be stupid." Andy said obviously sensing what Kyle had felt. The tone of his voice and the look on his gaunt face spoke of his tiredness and what he said almost sounded sarcastic.

Standing in a room full of rotting pieces of people with an obese monster that had become a god of a dying world, Kyle decided that destroying The Mouth was his only choice. The look on Andy's tired face told him that there would be no resistance from his brother.

The Mouth opened its disturbingly huge jaws. Massive lips peeled back exposing a grotesque and massive set of blood-stained teeth and it let out a strange and awful roar. Despite being immobile from gluttony, Kyle had to remember that this thing had majority control of whatever power this world had left.

Spinning on his heels, Kyle slapped both his palms on the wall behind him but his palms simply sank into something warm and soft. He had forgotten that the walls were completely covered with The Mouth's flesh. As quickly as he could he removed his palms, just in time to prevent another, more direct assault from the Mouth.

With a strange smile that made the sagging flesh on its face wrinkle and exposed its giant horse-like teeth, The Mouth scratched at Kyle's brain looking for another way in, another weakness. With each attack, Kyle had gotten better at shutting his brain but it made critical thinking nearly impossible and right now, as he scanned the huge room for some kind of exit, he needed his brain more than ever. He couldn't think, though, every time he tried to come up with an escape or an attack he felt The

Mouth's mental fingers inside his head and he knew that if he let him in again it would finish the job this time.

Almost out of sheer desperation, Kyle allowed his basest instincts to take over his actions. Like a frightened, caged animal he started darting around the room, his feet slipping on flesh, rot, and filth.

As the expression on Andy's face turned to confusion The Mouth watched curiously like a cat watching the death throes of its quarry. There was no worry in its huge eyes as it watched Kyle run from one corner to the other, from one pile of bones and body parts to another. There was no escape and once it got back into his head it would use every final ounce of power it had to shut his brain down.

Kyle's heart raced furiously as he searched. He may have looked like a panicked mouse trying to escape a cage but there was a purpose behind it. Rounding a large pile of half-eaten, rotting body parts his foot caught a brownish puddle and he fell backward. It would have been a hard, painful fall if not for The Mouth's squishy flesh. Lying on his back, covered in a foulness that would be impossible to describe, he found something that satisfied his "fight" instinct. Without hesitation, he grabbed a two-foot long piece of bone from the bottom of the pile he had fallen next to. The bone was clean of flesh, hollow as the marrow had long ago rotted away, and one end had been broken leaving a jagged, pointed end.

The bone had once been the right femur of a wedding photographer from Milwaukee named Al Donaldson. Up until now, that thirty-six-year-old bone had only helped support the leg of a lonely alcoholic, it was about to be used in a way that its original owner could have never imagined.

As Kyle scrambled to pick himself up he could feel The Mouth realize his plans and he could feel the monster's instant panic. The attempts by The Mouth to tear down his brain's defenses became more intense than ever and it took everything that Kyle had to stave them off. His face grimaced with the effort of keeping the powerful beast from shutting down his brain as he ran, full force, into the nearest wall and began stabbing the soft flesh furiously.

As The Mouth roared with a sound that hurt Kyle's ears and caused Andy to cup his hands over his, the mental battering ram on Kyle's brain ended. His arm was nearly a blur as he continued to stab and slash with Al Donaldson's femur. Thick, black fluid like overused, diesel motor oil flowed from each wound and sprayed in a wide swath around Kyle as the hollow bone collected the liquid. The flesh, in a radius equal to the length of Kyle's arm, was now hanging off of the wall in long jagged strips and he would have continued stabbing but the stench emanating from the black liquid that poured from the flaps of torn flesh was overwhelming.

Kyle fell to his knees and violently dry-heaved. It was entirely uncontrollable, the smell was something his olfactory had never sensed before and it made the sickening smell of rot seem as beautiful as the scent of a rose. In this position, his stomach convulsing, his head screaming with pain, his body tired, he felt pushed to his very limit and the thought of just giving in flashed across his mind. He was covered in rotting flesh and a black fluid that smelled worse than anything he could ever imagine, he wanted to just collapse and let it end. As if in response, the image of Poe eclipsed any other thought. This wouldn't be how he died, not in this strange chaos. It was the feeling of The Mouth gripping his mind for a brief moment that finally got him to his feet. The Mouth was now composed of a lot of flesh so Kyle had only injured a small part and it was now recovered and angry enough to renew its attempts on him. His entire torso heaving with labored breaths and his heart pumping nearly as quickly as it could, he looked into the horrific face of The Mouth, its satisfied grin was now replaced with a look of pure fury.

The Mouth had become comfortable with the power it siphoned from the world it was slowly consuming and had become immobile from the flesh it consumed but Al Donaldson's shattered femur, held in Kyle's fist, knew nothing of power, it was only a tool, a crude weapon. Reaching a point where he'd be unable to hold The Mouth's mental attacks at bay, Kyle gathered what little energy he had left and rushed toward that huge head that protruded from the mass of flesh that he called The Mouth. As if time itself slowed down around him, he felt every footfall and felt every heartbeat pulse in the fist that was tightly gripping the gore-covered femur. He cocked that femur in a strike position out at his side as The Mouth made a final, desperate attempt to enter his mind. Defenses down, it would only be a moment before The Mouth mentally crushed his brain so he didn't hesitate as he shoved the jagged end of his weapon into The Mouth's left eye. With a sick ease, the bone slid through the large eye and into what was beyond. He could feel the sensation of it "popping" through each successive layer of flesh, muscle, and sinew. The momentum spent, the bone was buried so far into The Mouth's head that only the couple inches where he had been gripping it was left sticking out. Like the open end of a broken pipe, the hollow bone began pouring out black fluid and visible chunks of whatever was in the center of The Mouth's head. After a few shudders that started with its massive head and spread into the flesh behind it, causing it to shake grotesquely, The Mouth was still. Kyle stood back from the gushing head. He swayed with fatigue as he looked to Andy, (who only stared with no visible emotion) and finally collapsed.

Nineteen

"I don't think it's going well in there," Otto said as he stared into the sky.

The thick clouds that had been blanketing the sky were now undulating like the angriest, upside-down sea. Twisting, spinning, and heaving, the maroon sky moved in a manner that could not translate to anything good. The wind, something that hadn't been felt by this world in a long time, had picked up severely also, giving life to the once calm sea that Otto, Darla, and Poe were waiting next to.

"It doesn't matter. We'll all die here anyway. I'm not even sure what Kyle thinks he's going to accomplish in there." Darla responded angrily.

"Shut up! Just fucking shut up!" Poe said as she rose from the beach and turned toward Darla. Darla only stared back defiantly with a look on her face that said 'I'm right, you'll see'. "We should be in there helping him anyway."

Otto didn't really want to get involved but provided a meek response anyway, "I don't think we'd find a way in and if we did I don't think we'd be much help." Poe's response was a look of dissension.

"What happens if he succeeds? Ever thought about that? You're just gonna take the next plane back to the good ol' U.S.A.?" Darla said as if to say that she wouldn't be shushed.

Pissed, Poe started to march from the beach toward the huge building where Kyle was confronting The Mouth. "Fuck both of you, I'm going up there."

Otto fired a glance of scold toward Darla and started after Poe, Darla stayed seated where she was. Unsure of her plan, he only followed next to Poe as she trudged quickly toward the big building on the hill.

"C'mon Poe, I know Darla can be a little rough but what are we going to do when we get up there?" Otto asked, a little afraid of what the response would be.

Poe glanced up at Otto without breaking her stride, gave the question some thought, then replied, "I don't know. I just feel like I should be doing something to help. If I'm going to be stuck in this shitty world forever I at least want it to be with Kyle alive. You don't ha….." She trailed off realizing that Otto had stopped listening and was staring straight up. Following his gaze, her mouth fell open. The sky was calming and the layer of clouds was quickly dissipating and clearing. The world around them was becoming considerably brighter as patches of a brilliantly bright, red sky were revealed.

"What the hell?" Otto asked softly to himself.

Within moments the sky was almost completely clear and the dull maroon light they were all used to was now a bright red. To Poe it made everything look like a cheap prop from an old film, where the desolate, red landscape is supposed to be Mars. The wind that had picked up died down also as her long hair fell lifeless to her shoulders again.

"Ummmm, Poe. Look!" Otto said urgently.

Poe removed her eyes from the bright sky and looked toward the building on the hill, expecting to see another wave of the long-armed creatures but there were none. Instead, she saw the entire building buckling and tilting before it finally imploded in a violent cloud of dust and flying debris. The destruction of the huge structure could be felt in the ground slightly where they were standing and a few small chunks flew far enough to disturb the ground near them. "No." The word fell from Poe's lips as her legs turned to worthless columns of jelly and she fell to the ground.

Otto walked up behind Poe and placed a consoling hand on the top of her head. He stared, awestruck , searching for something to say. Every attempt he made to offer comfort died once the words hit his lips. The top of the hill was still shrouded in a growing mass of dust, only the two strange towers still stood above the destruction. When he had felt that sufficient time had passed he held out his hand to Poe, "We should head back down to Darla, go back to the cave and decide what we should do next."

"We should go up there! What if he's trapped in there?" Poe asked breathlessly as tears began streaming down her face. "He might still be alive."

"Poe..." Otto said softly and calmly. "C'mon, look at that place. No one could survive that... we felt it all the way over here."

Without a word, Poe took Otto's hand and rose to her feet. She glanced back at the hill that now seemed so empty without the building where she had first met Kyle. With him gone she really had nothing left in this alien world, the thought of living out her days in this awful, red place made her more depressed than she ever thought she was capable of feeling. She didn't want to return to the cave, she didn't want to do anything. She felt as if all energy had left her body and all that she'd be capable of was curling into a ball and dissolving into the dirt.

"What the hell happened?" Darla asked as Poe and Otto walked up.

"No idea. The sky cleared up and then that building fell in." Otto responded despondently.

Poe continued walking, beyond Otto and Darla, until her feet were immersed in the water of the sea that was now painted bright red from the reflected sky. The beach house sat just to her left, another silent reminder of Kyle. Small waves lapped at her ankles as she hoped over and over in her mind that she would wake and find that this had all been some terrible nightmare or hallucination. She then wondered if it would hurt much if she simply walked into the sea until her feet couldn't touch bottom anymore, let the sea fill her lungs. She was too afraid to actually try it but it was a thought and she wondered how long it would take this place to motivate her to actually do it. With her feet in the water, her mind flashed with weak, random images that she knew weren't her own. A strange feeling of joy seemed to be spreading within her, this feeling wasn't hers either.

A scratching sound that seemed to come from the beach house broke the quiet and interrupted Poe's thoughts. Curiously she crept toward the windowless building, her head turned in an attempt to catch more of what she was hearing. The noise reminded her of when she was a young girl and would visit her grandmother. Her grandmother's home was old and mice often made their home in the empty walls. She hated trying to sleep there as she listened to the scritch-scratch of their claws. The sound she was hearing now was similar but sounded like a hundred mice navigating the insides of the walls. She placed her hand on the rough wall of the beach house and could feel the sound, it felt as if whatever was making the noise was trying to get out. She began to back away as the sound increased its speed and volume. Small cracks began to snake their way across the large walls like trails of lightning and Poe quickened her pace. Once the chunks of the wall began to break away and fall into the water she was able to see what had been making the scratching noises. It was tiny worms. Her mind flashed with the nightmare of what had happened to Tom. Worms began to spray and cascade out of every opening in the wall and Poe was now almost running backward through the shallow water. Horrified at what she was seeing she stopped at a spot on the beach once she had decided that she had put enough distance between herself and the crumbling building filled with little, wriggling worms. The building finally lost enough structural integrity that it completely fell away in huge chunks that sent up massive sprays of water and worms. A rounded, moving pile of worms nearly the size of the building itself was left in its wake. Poe watched as the pile flattened, greyish sheets of worms spread in every direction even into the depths of the water. There was nowhere she could go to escape them, she could run but she knew that wouldn't even work, they were moving quickly. Instead, she simply stood her ground on the beach. As a fast-moving sheet of worms approached her feet she winced as if in anticipation of a slap but the worms simply wriggled over her feet without pause. They continued past her and disappeared into the landscape. The pace of her heart began to slow as the few remaining worms disappeared into the world and then were completely gone. Not far up the beach behind her came a scream that she figured had to be Darla. Turning from the water, she ran to where she had last seen Otto and Darla.

"Are you guys okay?" Poe asked as she ran up to where Otto and Darla were standing, their backs were turned toward her and they were staring up the hill. "I heard you scream, Darla."

"That wasn't me." Darla turned and said as she thumbed toward Otto with her one good arm. "That was pussy-boy over here. A shit ton of worms just wiggled past us and he freaked out."

Poe couldn't help letting a tiny laugh escape her as Otto turned around and offered no defense, only a guilty, sheepish look. "They all came out of that building that was on the beach. It was gross." Poe said as she motioned toward the heaped ruins of the beach house.

"It was super gross!" Otto added.

With a hearty slap to Otto's broad back, Darla began to walk, "We should head up to the cave, I've had enough for one day. And there better not be any fucking worms in there."

Otto and Poe silently followed Darla back up the hill that led to their cave. As they walked, Poe thought she could feel the world changing or at least felt the world anticipating some big change. It wasn't a bad feeling so she took that to mean that the big change would be a good one. She wasn't sure if she could actually sense the absence of The Mouth or if she was simply assuming it. Either way, she felt this alien world, the world that would cease to be alien and would now be her home, getting stronger in some way.

***

Still within the lair of The Mouth, not long after Poe was pulled from the sea by Otto, Kyle grabbed his brother by the throat and started to drag him toward the wall that was only covered in ragged strips of shredded flesh. They passed the motionless head of The Mouth with the hollow bone still pouring a syrupy, black liquid onto the floor.

"You think you killed him don't you?" Andy said, forcing his words past Kyle's fist. "Use your brain, does he *feel* gone? Of course not, whatever he was he existed more mentally than he did physically."

Kyle tightened his grip on Andy's windpipe to try and silence him. It was true, though, he could feel it. It wasn't over. He was still new to this world and it's unseen, mental powers. He just wanted out of The Mouth's sick dungeon, get back to Poe. With Andy continuing on about the invisible powers of the world around them and Kyle's lack of understanding of these powers, Kyle placed his free, right palm on as much of the wall as he could. Nothing happened. Andy was distracting him, getting into his head.

"Shut up!" Kyle shouted as he released Andy's throat and slapped both palms on the wall. He closed his eyes and concentrated, trying to block out the fear and uncertainty of what was to come. He tried to find that power he had felt when on the other side of the wall. The feeling wasn't quite as strong as before but it was there. With a concentrated thought, a large section of the wall blew outward in chunks and dust. Unseen, covered beneath The Mouth's flesh, cracks ran throughout the room like the branches of an old tree. The huge room moaned from its damage. Aware of what he had just done, he wrapped his hand around Andy's throat again and they both exited through the ragged hole he just created.

Kyle dragged Andy about fifty yards, through the dirt, away from the deteriorating building. His brother trying the entire time to say something. From this vantage point they could easily see the quickly expanding cracks as they coursed over the walls. It took only moments for the structural integrity of the building to reach the point of collapse, and collapse it did, in spectacularly violent fashion. Kyle quickly determined that fifty yards was still too close to the huge building as it collapsed into itself. An expanding cloud of dust grew toward them and large chunks rained down around them. They both raised their arms in an attempt to shield themselves in the couple moments that it took for the building to complete its destruction.

Kyle had hoped that crushing what remained of The Mouth would completely destroy it but, in his mind, he knew that he hadn't. The Mouth may have been a cancer on this place but it had also become a piece of the world and just destroying the physical part wasn't enough.

"How the fuck did you do that?!" Andy screamed, his voice harsh from Kyle using his throat as a carrying handle. "How was that possible?"

Kyle brushed some dust and rocks from his messy, filthy hair. "It's a long story. This place and I are like this." Kyle said and he held up his dirty index and middle finger crossed together. "What do I have to do? How do I kill it?" Kyle asked Andy as they sat up, he was wholly unable to hide the frustration and desperation in his voice.

Andy only glanced at Kyle with the tired look of someone that was wishing they had been in that building when it came down, "I honestly don't know. You obviously weakened him, that I can feel, but he's still here. He's going to be super pissed."

For a few moments, Kyle only stood, covered in dust, surrounded by the detritus that only moments ago had been a building. His mind and body were both near exhaustion and he doubted he could take much more before he finally just gave in.

"Take us back," Kyle said to Andy with the suddenness that comes with a brilliant, new idea.

"I can't. He *let* me sleep, believe me, I would love to sleep but as long as he still has power, I can't sleep. I.....god I can't" Andy said with frustration. "I can still feel him... he's still in my head."

Kyle stared at the ground and searched his tired brain for any other ideas. Finally coming up with nothing he thrust both of his hands into the dirt around him and felt a connection like the mental equivalent to grabbing an electric fence. It was at the same time that he noticed the patches of clear, red sky above him that he felt some of the original strength of the world had returned and this alleviated at least a small amount of his fear. There was still the feeling of something awful just beyond the shadows, though, he had injured his prey but that prey was now in hiding and collecting its strength. As his adrenaline slowly wore off, he wondered if The Mouth felt nearly as run-down as he did, he wondered if the awful creature could sense his growing weakness. Hope was beginning to fade again.

Twenty

Poe stared at a point where the sea touched the perfect, red sky. Her thoughts of Kyle were interrupted only for a moment as she took notice of the beauty the world around her had taken on. It was a marked improvement over the dull maroon she had been used to. Despite the sunset-like beauty this world now had, she still longed for home. She had already given up on ever seeing a blue sky again but she still had some hope that Kyle would return. Her hair flitted around her dirty face from a light breeze that had a stale hint of something dead within it. She ignored the smell with the thought that this world's air had been stagnant for longer than she cared to guess, she figured the entire world probably needed to air out. Standing above the gently rolling sea, she grasped the bare rock that stuck up in front of her. It was her hope that she had developed enough of a connection with the world that she'd be able to get some answers but all she got were random images that made no sense to her. When she had "heard" (or maybe felt) the voice that spoke to her of Kyle's dream, the connection through the water must have been a fluke, or a one-time deal, either way, she was far from seeing things the way Kyle was able to. She had decided she wouldn't take her palms from the rock until Kyle returned or she knew for sure that he was gone, just in case.

"I don't think everything is quite okay yet." The voice coming from behind Poe was Darla as she squeezed out of the cavern. "I've never seen things like this, the breeze is great, but It still doesn't feel…safe."

Poe didn't respond but understood what she meant. It was the same feeling she would feel when she was a kid and could see a storm approaching. She was scared to death of thunderstorms, so when she'd see those black clouds approaching her stomach would bunch into knots.

Standing next to Poe, Darla continued, " I still don't think we can really do anything but I hate just hanging out. Something has changed, for the better, but I don't think it's over. We should go see what's left of that building. I have to do something to take my mind off of this stupid arm... fuck it hurts."

"I agree," Poe replied as she stared into Darla's eyes to let her know how serious she was. "I would have gone up there right away."

With a nod, Darla turned toward the cavern entrance and yelled, "Hey Otto! We're leaving! Let's go!"

With no knowledge of what they would walk into and with little care, the three of them made their way back down their hill. The few hours or so that they spent resting from the battle had seemed like enough to all of them. Although they knew that if they were to encounter The Mouth or any of his long-armed monsters they wouldn't last long, this was their last stand. Whatever remained of The Mouth's building, whatever was waiting for them on the beach, they would do whatever they could, as little as it may be. They were tired, their muscles ached with fatigue, and their pale friends from the sea had long retreated. This was that old, noble notion that, if they had to go down, they'd go down with a fight.

As the trio silently walked within sight of the destroyed beach house, Darla stopped them by throwing her arm out. She turned back to Poe and Otto and pointed to two figures standing next to the pile of rubble that had been the beach house. They were still too far away to tell exactly what they were seeing but there were definitely two things standing on the beach. Slowly, Darla led the march closer.

"It's Kyle!" Poe nearly screamed once they got close enough to make out Kyle and Andy standing, staring at the destroyed beach house.

Before Darla could even react, Poe was running as fast as her tired legs could carry her toward Kyle. He turned and smiled just as Poe nearly tackled him by throwing her arms around his neck. Without a word or a pause, she kissed him as hard as she could on the mouth and he kissed her back with the same enthusiasm. They stood in the embrace for a moment and for that time nothing mattered, though things would matter soon.

"What the fuck happened up there?!" Poe asked as she pushed herself off of Kyle and stared at him seriously. "And seriously you stink... really, really bad."

Taking a moment to collect his thoughts with Poe, Otto, Darla, and Andy all staring and waiting to see what his response would be, Kyle finally answered. "First, Poe saved me from myself, then I stabbed that asshole up there with a bone." No one moved or changed their expression after his simple answer so he added, "Then I brought the building down to finish the job. I don't think it's over, though... that piece of shit is still here."

"I don't think any of you idiots know how connected to this world he was. All you succeeded in doing was pissing him off. He will be back and soon." Andy said with a seriousness that almost sounded angry.

The five of them stood on the beach, most of them were fully aware of the gravity of their situation and they all were nearly convinced that they would soon be dead. It was that realization, that inevitability that gave them courage, it didn't mean they wouldn't try and live, it just meant that they were okay with it as long as they made a mess on their way out.

"So how do we kill somethin' that doesn't exist?" Otto asked genuinely, he sounded tired and frustrated.

No one answered, instead they each looked around as if the answer would be written somewhere near them. After a few moments of thinking, all eyes landed on Andy.

With a laugh that lasted a little too long, Andy said, "I was just a fucking errand boy. I don't know how this goddamn place works. He got into....no, IS in my head, that's all I know." His eyes getting wider with every word he turned to his brother, "Kyle seems to have a better understanding of this shit-hole than I do. I've been here for... I don't fucking know... a long time and I can't make a building fall like that."

It was then that Poe remembered her strong mental connection when she entered the sea. Kyle already had a strong connection so if he went in it would now only get stronger. She looked into Kyle's eyes and said, "Get into the water."

"What?" Kyle asked with a look of confusion.

Poe thought for a moment that she could try and explain to Kyle that somehow it was the water along with something that had grown within her that allowed her to warn him in his "dream" but she didn't want to take the time. Suddenly she instead placed both her palms on Kyle's chest and shoved him with all the strength she had. With a look of surprise written on his face he tumbled backward and fell into the sea. Immediately she regretted the act and even wondered what would possess her to do it. If anything she wanted to grab him and find a place to hide together. As he hit the water hard she suddenly felt as if it hadn't been her decision at all to shove him.

Without warning, Kyle disappeared beneath the surface of the water, it wasn't particularly deep but just enough depth to consume him. He would have thought that the sensation he felt in the moment he went under was death had it been his first time having his brain connect with an entire world. This time, the connection consumed all that he was. He had gotten much better at regulating the door in and out of his brain but being suddenly shoved into the water completely caught him off-guard and that door was violently forced completely open. If anyone was there to ask he would have described it as an out of body type experience. Thoughts and feelings became intertwined and physical sensation disappeared. He wasn't used to existing only as a thought, being forced into it was overwhelming. He suddenly felt like he was tumbling without direction through a space that was entirely new to him. It was The Mouth that steadied him. He could feel The Mouth, could sense him. The sensation was like crawling through a dark basement knowing that there was something there, something that wanted to kill you. With all of himself that he was able to fully control, he searched for that evil thing almost in the same way someone searches their memory for an acquaintance's name. It didn't take long to "see" it. In this place The Mouth felt massive, a mountain-sized shadow looming in the corner of the basement. He approached the shadow with all the confidence of a comic book hero. He walked until he felt consumed by the vast shadow, it was here that he felt fingers on him. Everything was dark so he couldn't see what felt like hundreds of groping, poking fingers. They were pushing, pulling him deeper within the shadow. He felt a calm as he gave into the will of the fingers around him, he was becoming a part of the darkness.

Like a drug trip from hell, Kyle's mind, his very being coalesced with what was left of The Mouth. On a plane that was made purely of thought and feeling he felt the ancient evil of the beast, felt it not just surround him but enter him in a way not even the worms had. He could feel the desperation and panic of a powerful monster that was in its death throes, he could also feel fear but that seemed to be his own. A part of him reactively struggled to escape this new horror but, instead of yielding to this instinctual act of self-preservation, he tried plunging deeper within the evil.

Like two hurricanes merging, Kyle and The Mouth swirled together in the hypothetical. One a demented evil of forgotten age the other a twenty-eight year old slacker from Wisconsin. Kyle could feel himself merging so completely he was starting to lose track of what thoughts and feelings were his own and which were The Mouth's, the feeling was horrible but he felt that the deeper he got within the creature the better chance he had at destroying it. He knew he was losing control though, The Mouth had been much more powerful and definitely was able to control this world's power with more skill than Kyle.

Sudden horror struck Kyle, a physical feeling of pain consumed him with an intensity he'd never felt before. The pain ripped him violently from the mental showdown he was in. His awakening was in slow motion and the moment he opened his eyes was like a frozen snapshot, if only for a moment. In that moment of waking he was airborne, being ripped from the water by a pale one, large droplets of blood and water hung around them. Once the moment of slow motion ended they landed hard onto the dry beach. As Poe screamed behind them, the pale one sat on him and stared down with its black eyes as its flesh wings folded onto its back.

Darla, Poe, and Otto were poised to rip the pale one sitting atop Kyle into tiny, pale pieces the moment they flew out of the water if it weren't for Nigel and, what looked like, the entire rest of the pale ones left alive. The water seemed almost alive with all the winged creatures emerging. As they rose from the water they folded in their wings and walked toward the beach.

"Stop! Please. We are sorry for our methods but this was the only way." Nigel said, not even fully emerged from the water.

Looking down at Kyle he continued, "Kyle would have made a perfect vessel for that creature, we had to remove him from there....the force was necessary. He was being consumed. There is nothing you can do now.....I am very...very sorry."

The pale one that forcibly removed Kyle from the water stood up and backed away to join the rest of its kind. Kyle was bleeding heavily from his ears and eyes. Poe and Darla descended on him.

"Otto, give me your shirt!" Darla yelled. Without hesitation or protest, he removed his shirt and tossed it to her.

Trying her hardest to tear the shirt into strips she bit down on part of the shirt and tried tearing with her good arm. Now realizing what her intentions were Otto snatched the shirt back from her and easily started ripping it into wide, ragged pieces. Taking the strips of fabric from him, Darla tightly wrapped Kyle's head in hopes of stopping the blood that was beginning to soak into his wet shirt turning it varying shades of pink. Poe couldn't help but cry as she knelt down to help Darla. Kyle just grimaced and screamed with pain as they tied strips around him and the ground beneath him grew darker as it soaked up more of his blood.

"Again, I am sorry. My friend's action was to bring Kyle back, things could have been made worse. We had to act." Nigel said solemnly as chaos unfolded on the beach in front of him, he wasn't sure anyone was listening. "I honestly had hoped we could have gotten him out in time. I do believe though that Kyle's death also means the death of the evil."

Poe sobbed as Darla frantically tried to stem the bleeding, it was a battle she was losing. Kyle's cries began to grow fainter and weaker with each passing moment. His skin was nearly as pale as the creature's that rose from the sea. Poe cradled his head in her hands and looked into his half-open, rolling eyes.

"I love you, Kyle." She said, her voice shaking badly. "Oh... my god... I'm... so sorry. I don't know... why. I..."

With what seemed like an immense amount of effort, Kyle steadied his eyes on Poe's and answered, "I... Lo..ve. You....... too. I'm.... sor....ry. I guess... I...I'm.. no.. hero." He tried hard to force a small laugh but couldn't.

As a tremor of sadness rose from her belly and she only just barely resisted the desire to bawl uncontrollably, she forced a small smile and said, "You have nothing.. to be sorry for.. Please, I can't lose you again."

Kyle's eyes began rolling and closing like someone on the verge of falling asleep. Rivers of blood poured from his eyes like bright red tears but most of it was pouring from his ears, he summoned all the strength he had and lifted a blood-covered hand to place on Poe's face. He forced his eyes open, and said, "Get ho… me. Lea….. ve this.. place. I'll be…. okay."

"I'm not leavin…." Poe began but stopped as Kyle's hand fell from her face and his eyes closed.

"Poe. It is time to go. Now." Nigel said from just behind her. "Kyle is gone."

Kyle's body was limp and lying in a pool of mud made from dirt and blood but Darla continued working on stemming the flow of blood. Poe leaned forward and kissed his cold lips.

Nigel placed a hand on Poe's shoulder and repeated what he had just said. Slowly, Poe rose. She had given into the desire to bawl now. An incredible sadness and hopelessness had overcome her as she watched Darla and Otto work on Kyle's pale body. She turned toward Nigel, if Kyle was gone then going home would be the only thing keeping her from just letting the sea fill her lungs and take her. "You know how I can leave?"

Nigel furrowed his brow and answered, "I do. You will have just one chance." Turning toward Darla and Otto he asked, "Do either of you wish to return?" The only answer he would receive from the blood-covered, exhausted pair was a dismissive look that meant they were going to stay.

"How the hell is she going to just leave? You stupid, creepy freak.." Andy walked up and asked.

Nigel turned toward Andy and, without a word he raised his right hand. A short, broad, sharp looking spike of bone rose out at the base of his palm. He shoved the spike into Andy's abdomen just below the ribs. Andy's face contorted with horror and confusion as he looked into Nigel's face. With a jerk, he removed his spike and allowed Andy to fall to the beach. "Lie with him, Poe. This is your chance. He is about to fall asleep for the last time. For all you have done, Andy…"

Horrified but somehow understanding what she had to do, Poe laid herself next to Andy and put her arm around his thin, twitching frame. As Andy's moans turned to muted gargles, she never took her eyes off of Kyle. It seemed to only take a few moments before the bright, red sky above her and the barren world around her began to ebb and fade. She wasn't sure if she was seeing things correctly or if it had been a trick of her departure but just before everything went black and she felt her consciousness slip, she swore that she saw Kyle's limp body consumed by a mass of worms.

Twenty-One

The feeling of waking from a nightmare with the knowledge that it had actually all been real was one that Apollonia was completely familiar with. She woke up from her nightmare with her arm draped over an emaciated, dead body. Before she even opened her aching eyes she knew that she had returned home. The smell of green, of trees, of grass, and flowers filled her sinuses gloriously and with the hint of a smile she opened her eyes. Above her was the clear, bright, blue sky of early evening. She rubbed her painful, tired eyes and rose from the ground. She appeared to be in a park somewhere. Leaving Andy's lifeless body, she walked past a weathered picnic table and up to a clearing in the thick trees that surrounded her. She was high up above a city. Beyond the huge, forested hill she was on was a body of water and a large, green bridge. She wasn't immediately sure of where she was but she couldn't help but feel a sense of joy and relief at escaping that horrible world. Covered in dried blood, her clothes tattered and stained, she turned to find a hiking trail that would lead her off the hill. Part of her felt bad for leaving Andy's body but after what she had just been through the feeling wasn't enough to make her so much as turn back. The theater of her mind was replaying the last time she and Kyle were face to face causing an emotional conflict of jubilation to be home and incredible sadness at losing Kyle. She wasn't sure she'd ever be able to live the life she had left, things would definitely be different now, forever.

A middle-aged couple from South Carolina were the first people to see Poe, they were visiting their son and decided to check out Portland's Forest Park. The young girl they had found was covered in blood and filthy. She didn't say much so they decided to just dial 911 and let the Portland police figure out what the girl's story was, luckily the couple hadn't walked far enough to find Andy's almost alien looking body.

In the weeks that followed her return Poe would be interviewed by numerous detectives but, knowing the truth would just get her thrown into a mental institution or years of therapy, she gave no explanation for her six-month absence, she didn't even tell her tale to her overjoyed parents. All that she gave them was that she didn't remember anything, she didn't know where the blood on her clothes had come from or who the dead body in the park was.

The blood they found on her clothing didn't match the John Doe they found in the park so she would eventually be released from custody for lack of any actual reason to hold her. She then had to endure reporter microphones shoved in her face and an almost constant media presence outside her apartment door for months. Her mystery "story" made her a minor celebrity for a short while and everyone waited for her to come out with some shocking tale of kidnapping or alien abduction. There were even a couple "true crime" shows that ran her odd story.

She never spoke another word about where she had been and her fame faded quickly. It wasn't long before she found herself completely alone. Trials were held, tests were performed, but in the end nothing conclusive could be proven and Apollonia simply faded away.

She had spent so much time dreaming of being back in her own world beneath that beautiful blue sky but, now that she was back, all she could think about was Kyle. She missed him terribly and every day was filled with a gut-twisting regret for leaving him. Even the most beautiful of days felt just as miserable as when she was beneath that dim, maroon sky. Her strong desire to not be alone drove her to move in with her parents for a while but their almost constant and justified concern for her eventually led her to move out on her own.

Living in a tiny apartment, all she could afford on the string of medial jobs she kept starting and leaving, she quickly realized that she had lost her taste for pretty much everything. The things she once loved now couldn't hold her interest, it was as if the world through her eyes had lost all color.

Three months had passed since she woke on that hill in Oregon when the reoccurring dream began. In it, she was flying above an alien looking landscape with a familiar, bright red sky. The ground beneath her was almost completely covered in plants of practically every color, structures of varying shape and size stuck up randomly from the growth. As she flew, the plants gave way to a rocky beach with small waves lapping against it. She flew over a gently rolling sea, ruby in color from the sky's reflection. Like a small island, a cone-shaped mountain protruded from the waves and at its hollow pinnacle sat the visage of a man in a light, billowy robe. It was Kyle. She immediately thought about how long his hair was getting as the breeze played with it. As she flew by she wanted so badly to speak to him, to touch him but he only continued to stare out over the sea. As Kyle and that rocky cone disappeared behind her she awoke. She was filled with a mixture of joy for seeing her love and sadness for the realization that it was only a dream. It would be a dream she would never, ever forget mostly because it was a dream that she would have over and over again.

Epilogue

Jack awoke slowly. As he opened his sleep-weary eyes he seemed aware of a sensation that he hadn't felt in a long time. It was a warmth on his face that only sunshine could bring. For a brief moment that could only occur within the first seconds of waking he questioned his most recent memories and he half expected to find himself sitting up in his own bed. The sensation that the rough floor he had been sleeping on brought, along with the acrid smell of his prison quickly dispelled any fantasy of waking up at his home.

As his eyes slowly adjusted to the bright light that had warmed his face he sat up, Sandi still stirring sleepily in his lap. What he saw almost instantaneously erased all traces of sleep from his mind. The small, round room that had held him and his wife for an undetermined amount of time was brightly illuminated with a light that could only be described as sunlight. It wasn't the sunlight he'd always known, it was strange, redder. The area of wall where Andy would make his entrance was now a large, jagged hole that was bright with that wonderful light.

"Sandi! Look!" Jack said, the tone of his voice rising quickly with excitement.

Sandi groaned, rubbed her tired eyes, and looked up at Jack curiously. "What?" She asked but she needed no answer. As her eyes adjusted she realized that their awful room was illuminated like it had never been.

Jack rose from the floor leaving Sandi sitting beneath him with a look of disbelief illuminated on her face. In front of him, beyond the large hole in the wall, was a landscape that took away his breath. The room that held them was obviously high up, giving him an expansive view of the land below. Standing silhouetted at the opening in their room he looked out at what looked like a barren, fallow desert with an incredibly bright, red sky. Walking right up to the edge of their prison he felt a breeze tease the growing scraps of what was left of his hair. He breathed deep, the smell that the breeze carried was awful yet he thought he could feel something good in it. He looked down, it was only then that he realized how high above the ground they really were.

"Where.... are... we?" Sandi asked the silhouette of her husband.

Turning from the bright opening in the wall, Jack answered, "Looks like we're in some kind of tower." He walked over to Sandi and helped her up from the floor. With a loving kiss to her forehead and a smile, he said, "I don't think Andy is coming back."

As if to see for herself, Sandi walked to the edge of their room. First, she looked out at the red tinged landscape before her, then she looked down. The thought that they may now be free felt incredible but the distance that she saw to the ground curbed her jubilation. "We must be a hundred feet up." She said as she turned back to Jack.

With a smirk, he approached her and took her in his arms. "I'd say more like two-hundred. I guess we'll have to find a way down."

A special thank you to:

Tarin Erickson

Sarah Clark

Amanda Morrill

Nathan Klinger

Eric Quade

If I've forgotten anyone just email me and I'll get you on the next one!